AIDY AWARD

Naughty Wolf/ Aidy Award. – 1st ed.

Cover by Jacqueline Sweet

For my own little brother

ACKNOWLEDGMENTS

Acknowledgements

Great big thanks on this book go to the coolest women who helped me plot this book. Hugs to Sylvia McDaniel, Peggy McKenzie, and Kat Kennedy.

This story is so much better because of you.

Super duper thanks to my Amazeballs, especially those that volunteered to help me proofread at the last minute.

Extra hugs to Sydney M Dolan-Neblett, Kerrie Moore, Tamye Whitener, Patricia Centlivre, Lisa Mathis, Jeanette Merrick, and Dorothy-Helen Billmeier!

I am very naughty
But in a very nice way

—KinkyQuotes.com

THE KOSTEST WITH THE MOSTEST

Kosta always loved pack mating ceremonies, as long as he wasn't the one getting mated. He was an expert level flirt, and more than one wolftress had tried their best to work their way into the sacred circle with him.

In the past, he'd taken a few of them home and made them howl at the moon with pleasure. Not this time. Not when fun and flirting had been replaced with fate.

Tonight's mating ritual was a whole new deal. His brother Maxsim decided to mate a human, of all things. A very beautiful human, who was smart, and sweet, and who had recently shifted into wolf form after being marked, and then eaten the face off a local pack alpha. Frankly, that asshat had it coming. Gal was a badass, but she wasn't one of them.

No way he could fault Maxsim for falling for the cute and curvy librarian his brother had a crush on since high school. Mating her was a whole other deal. Wolves mated wolves. So it had been for hundreds of years. The tradition kept the packs and the existence of their entire species secret and safe.

Biting a human, much less marking them with a mate's bite, was beyond taboo. Even revealing themselves as a wolf-shifter to a human could be punishable by death. At least it had been until the Wolf Tzar and the strong-armed reign of the Volkovs had been brought to an end. A mutiny spurred by Kosta's oldest brother, Niko, and his own mother, nonetheless.

Their mother, the revolutionary, and his broken, ghost-of-a-man brother had changed his whole damn world. Kosta wasn't sure he liked this new mish-mosh life they were living. Yet, here he stood, at a mating ceremony where wolves and humans were claiming their true mates. Like that was even a thing.

True mates, fated to be each other's one and only love. What bullshit.

He rubbed his chest where the ache for his carefree days pressed against his psyche. Days where he hunted in the woods, kept his pack safe by being the best Enforcer he could, and got to fuck around with any girl he liked.

"Isn't it beautiful?" A young wolftress sidled up to Kosta and sighed at the matings happening in the sacred circle. She was cute, with that nerdy look he had a thing for, but she had the dark hair and the blue eyes of a Troika pack member. He much preferred the springy blonde curls and chocolatey brown eyes of– fuck. He was comparing her to Heli.

Heli, the human woman he'd been dicking around with for the past few weeks. Heli, the luscious lady who always smelled like butter and brown sugar. Sweet, sensuous Heli, who had his cock hard as stone with just a look.

Shit. He was going to have to break it off with Heli. Just thinking about her was making him hard and she was a distraction. The Troikas were smack dab in the in the middle of a pack war. He couldn't afford one smidgen of his attention to waver.

"Kosta? Uh, isn't the mating ritual under the full moon beautiful?" The pretty little wolftress was trying so hard to get his attention and he was standing here daydreaming about break up sex with another woman. He was such an ass.

He turned his full attention to the woman by his side and flipped his flirt switch to maximum. He took her hand in his and kissed the inside of her wrist. "Indeed, it is. Why aren't you out there, sweet thing?"

Her eyes went as round as the moon. "Me?"

"Absolutely, you. Let's see who we can find for you to have a little romance with, shall we?" This was a game he had down to a science. He never wanted to hurt any wolftresses feelings, but he wasn't going to mate any of them. His father impressed upon him that the Troika boys' mates would be strategic matches to further ties with other packs. His mother believed he could choose to love who he wanted. Maybe he didn't want a mate at all, or maybe he'd already found her.

It was easy enough to place himself directly into the friend zone with this wolftress, with a whole lot of sex appeal and charm thrown in for fun. Now to find her a lucky wolf.

Aha. There, just a quarter of the way around the circle, he spotted s strapping young wolf with more than half a hard on. He had one arm across his chest and no game. That guy didn't think he could get a girl and this girl needed a guy. Bingo bango.

And the pack all thought his mother was the matchmaker.

He held out his hand to the wolftress and began humming. The girls always fell for the waltz. He put an arm around her back and together they danced their way around the sacred circle. Under any other circumstances, with this soft, lush wolftress in his arms, he'd give her a little taste, but not tonight. Kosta very carefully avoided the moonlight so it didn't appear to anyone he was bringing this woman into the mating ritual.

They quickly approached the wolf he had picked out for her and Kosta spun the little wolftress, letting her go right at the pivotal moment. No way was she going to recover out of that spin before she crashed right into shy wolf boy. In three, two... "Hey Sorkin, catch her."

One. Splat. Sorkin did the Troikas proud with a damn quick reaction time. The two still fell to the ground in a heap, but Sorkin cradled the sweet wolftress as they plummeted and protected her with his own body. She landed sprawled across him, their faces inches apart.

“Hi,” she giggled.

“Hello, there.” Sorkin sounded dumbstruck.

Perfect. Duty done.

Now time to high tail it out of there before any other wolftress set her sights on him. He’d make better time if he shifted, but this was his last pair of clean jeans. He’d already used his emergency change of clothes in the back of his truck. Laundry day had come and gone while he and Max had been on the hunt for lone Grimm pack members who weren't ready to come into the fold. More than a few didn't want Gal as their alpha.

No shifting for him. Walking back to his car it was then. He could keep himself out of sight and mind of any stragglers. Two yards into the forest and he knew he wasn’t alone.

"Why do you do that, Kos?" A quiet and broken voice came out of the shadows behind him.

It was a voice that a week ago he never thought he'd get to hear again. Niko leaned against the trunk of a tree, all but his glowing blue eyes hidden by the darkness.

Kosta slowly approached. Lord knew his brother was jumpy as fuck these days. "Do what?"

"Let go of all the girls who want you. She would have dropped to her knees right here in the shadows and sucked your dick if you'd so much as looked at her. She was hot and wet for you, couldn't you scent that on her?"

The scent in the air right now was bitterness, anger, and despair.

"Of course I could. Since when are you a love 'em and leave 'em wet jackass?" There was a lot about Niko that had changed. He wasn't the sunny eldest brother and heir to the pack anymore. That was hard for Kosta. He'd worshipped the ground Niko walked on for a long damn time.

This guy hiding in the dark wasn't the same man who'd left for Russia to serve the Wolf Tzar years ago.

"I left Zara nice and wet when I–" He cut his sentence short and turned his back on Kosta.

Shit. He shouldn't have pushed Niko. They were all lucky to have him back. Kosta didn't think he should have come to the mating ceremony tonight. But Selena, as the matriarch, had insisted. If the pack was going to accept Max as the alpha even though Niko had returned, he needed to be here to give his blessing. He'd done his duty.

Niko shrugged his shoulders and folded into himself. "Whatever. I'm going to Sleepy Folk to get a drink if anyone needs me. Not that they will."

“Okay, Eeyore,” Kosta said under his breath, although with their wolf senses, his brother would hear anyway.

Niko's only response to that was to give Kosta the finger. In a few more strides, Niko shed his clothes and dropped them in the dirt. Kosta waited for the pop of bones, stretching of skin, and prickle of fur as his brother shifted into his white wolf form.

He didn’t. Niko walked away through the trees on two legs. Naked.

A tingle of dread from his wolf's supernatural senses pushed at Kosta like knife pricks under his skin. They were going to have to talk to Doc about some psychological counseling for Niko. What the fuck?

Well, he’d seen more than enough naked asses for the night, thank you very much. He’d take the long way around. The Reserve was his second home, and he knew every nook and cranny, every fallen tree, every gopher hole. He’d spent more time running around these woods with his brothers and pack mates than he had in school.

Ten minutes later, that intimate knowledge came in handy when he spotted the hunting blind someone had tried to make out of underbrush and branches. Dammit. He'd been thinking about how they were going to bring Niko out of his darkness and hadn’t been paying attention to all the little cues his wolf senses were sending him.

A quick scent of the air and he identified two wolf-shifters. They weren’t Troikas and he didn’t know all the Grimms on sight yet, but he recognized the particular saltiness of the Bay pack. The East Coast sea wolves were as adept at hunting in the ocean as they were on land.

Kosta knew them to be bastard one-bloods. Thinking they were all superior and shit was disgusting. His own brother might be pushing his boundaries of what being a wolf meant, but he didn't command anyone to think or behave the way he did.

The Troikas brothers were raised in love, to know the

difference between right and wrong, and to stand up for what they believed in. Other wolves naturally gravitated to that kind of leadership. Even during this new pack war they'd created, Troika wolves were loyal.

Max was going to make a good alpha because he didn't have to throw his weight or fangs around for others to follow his lead. Kosta didn't have to worry about that. He wouldn't ever be the alpha of a pack. Not him or Niko.

That didn't mean he should stand around and do nothing when other alphas bullied the shifters and humans in their territory into subservience. Something rumored to be happening over at the Bay.

What made these two dumbasses think they could encroach on Troika territory on the most sacred of nights? It wasn't the first time another pack had sullied the Reserve since Niko had been accused of killing the Wolf Tzar. It would be the last time these two wolves in particular were going to leave their taint in his nose.

Kosta quietly stripped and hid his clothes on a low hanging branch and let his wolf out. His bones cracked, his vision changed so that he could easily see into the dark, and the fur pushed up out of his skin. He wanted to howl at the brilliance of the full moon that gave all of his kind her strength and love. He would, after he ripped out the throats of the intruders.

It was easy for him to stalk through the night with stealth. His wolf was the darkest black all over except for the glow of his eyes. He kept those hooded and hunted his prey.

The two shifters were upwind from him and the sacred circle. If this was the kind of training Bay gave their enforcers, they deserved to go down. They couldn't be easier to track and ensnare if they were fluffy white bunnies.

Just like those ridiculous bunny slippers Heli wore. She was completely adorable in them, which he'd never admit. When she was all satisfied and sleepy after he'd made her come a half dozen times, but insisted on getting up to pee before bed, she'd slip them on, even though she was stark naked, and shuffle across her room. So fucking cute.

Damn it. He should not be thinking about Heli's perfectly plump ass, swaying like it did, when he was on the hunt. Shit. He really, really needed to break up with her. Again.

He shook his head to clear it of those too tempting thoughts and reacquired his targets. Not only were they upwind, but they also jabbered away, and not as quietly as they probably thought they were. To top it off, one of them lit a cigarette.

"He's not coming. This was a stupid idea. Why would he come this way?" The non-smoker stomped his feet like they were falling asleep from standing around too long.

Smoker took a drag and flicked the ashes into the brush. "I don't know. I'm not going to question Decker's orders, are you?"

Decker. The new alpha of the Bay pack. His father, the previous alpha, had died only a few months ago. Decker must be trying to prove himself with these attacks on

Troika. Like they didn't have enough trouble already with the Crescent pack breathing down their necks.

Who were these two waiting for? Not their alpha. That guy was too incompetent to fight his own battles. No, he'd sent his dogs to do his work and test the Troika borders while their efforts were focused on incorporating the Grimms and defending against the Crescents.

There was one sure way to find out what they wanted. Scare it out of them.

Kosta crept around behind them, still completely unnoticed, and sat down. *Who are you waiting for, fellas? The big bad wolf?*

Non-smoker jumped about three feet, but smoker slowly turned, the cigarette hanging from his bottom lip.

You should put that out, before I put it out for you. And don't even think about littering in my forest.

Smoker plucked the lit cigarette from his lip, slipped it back into the box and shoved the whole thing, still smoking, into his pocket. He swallowed and said, "The alpha of the Bay pack would like to speak with you."

That did not merit a response more than a raised eyebrow.

"He thinks you may be of a mind to discuss the current state of affairs, unlike your brother."

Decker wants to negotiate his surrender? I accept.

"No, uh, he heard through his network that you were not happy about Maxsim mating a human and taking over the pack. He said to tell you, he empathizes and might be able to help you with that problem."

Problem? Seriously? Decker was dumber than Kosta thought if he even considered for a second that any Troika would betray the pack.

Having these two frightened emissaries that smelled of urine right here in front of him was too good an opportunity to get intel. It was almost a shame, too, because he would have fun ripping them limb from limb.

Tell me, does the Bay pack truly believe Wolves are superior to humans? That we are stronger, smarter, and inherently suited to rule over mankind as our servants?

He'd meant that to sound sarcastic, but the timid shifter didn't get that message.

He lit up and got all excited. "Yeah. Decker is changing the future, man. Wolves aren't going to have to hide in the dark anymore and we get all the women we want. I mean, well, the enforcers in the pack do. I don't mind the leftovers though. I'm getting more pussy now than I ever did before the pack war started. You could have your pick, not that you have to–"

Enough. This schmoe had eaten up every line Decker fed his pack, and then some. It wasn't that surprising he'd bought their loyalty with access to women. The Decker Kosta knew always was a degenerate.

The smoker glared at his buddy. "What my friend here is trying to say is, Decker appreciates that wolfkind has certain advantages of nature that humans do not, and he has used the current shift in the regime to use those to benefit the pack, and indeed all wolves. He would like if you would, ah, visit the Bay and see for yourself. He thinks you might like to make similar changes in Rogue."

That fucker. What Kosta would like to do is send Decker a couple of severed heads in a bag. What he needed to do was go tattle on Decker to Max so he and Gal could take care of the problem.

A tension, like claws on a chalkboard, rankled through him at that idea. His animal side whispered that he could eliminate the threat without Max ever knowing it existed in the first place. That's what Niko would do if he was his old self. Niko acted. Max thought, and Kosta followed along for the fun of it.

He was done having fun.

This was war.

You tell Decker I'll be there. He turned his back on the emissaries and nonchalantly walked away into the woods. It took only a minute for him to fade into the dark and then he turned and paid attention to what they did next.

"Holy shit. Decker was right," non-smoker whispered.

"Of course he was." Smoker looked out into the trees where Kosta had walked away, not being smart enough to even think he might have changed directions.

"We are going to get our pick of the ladies when we bring this news back. Come on. Let's get out of this creepy-ass forest and tell Decker we turned a Troika." The guy practically skipped through the woods.

Smoker was a bit more wary and looked over his shoulder one last time before following his dumb buddy. Kosta tracked them all the way to the far end of the

Reserve that butted up against a neighborhood. He made sure they got into that car and drove off without causing any more problems on Troika land.

Turned a Troika.

Complete horseshit, but also the perfect cover. He could slip into the Bay pack and dismantle it from the inside out before they could cause any more problems for the Troikas or the poor people of Bay. Sounded like Decker had already broken the cardinal rule to not let humans know who and what they were. The humans were probably terrified. Fuck. That was probably where they were getting the women non-smoker had talked about.

He had to do something about that. Not Max, not Niko. Him. He was going to save those people and take down the bad guy.

Any wolf worth his mettle could scent when someone was lying. He was really going to have to sell it, not just to Decker and the Bay pack, but to his own family. They were going to have to think he really was betraying them.

Shit. This was going to kill his mom. He'd work out how to manage that after he went to see Heli. First order of business was breaking up with her, followed by copious amounts of break up sex. He was going off to war after all and he could die. If he did, he wanted to die with a smile on his face.

Yep. Heli had to go. She was already too much of a distraction and he couldn't have her around him and the danger he was going into.

He'd fucking destroy every one-blood on the planet if

anything bad happened to his Heli. Even thinking about her anywhere near the Bay pack made him want to throw up. No, Heli needed to stay far, far away from those assholes. The best way to do that was to make sure she wanted to stay away from him.

Kosta decided to run to her house instead of going back for his car. He wasn't going to need clothes at Heli's house anyway. It took him only a few minutes to get to her house and he wasn't surprised to see the light coming from the back porch. Ever since the Grimms had attacked their house and her sister had gone missing, Heli had trouble sleeping.

There were only two things that helped her get her zzz's. Baking cookies, which he could smell she'd already done, and rough, ride 'em cowgirl sex. He was always happy to provide the latter.

He had to admit, it was kind of nice that he didn't have to hide his true nature from her. She'd found out exactly what he looked like the night Max became alpha and Heli's best friend Gal had turned into a wolf shifter too.

She had been surprised, but not scared of his wolf. She had even taken to scratching him behind the ears when he was in this form, which he secretly loved. Her touch did something to him every time. It either got him hard in an instant, or he went all soft and squishy on the inside.

Puppy love.

That's what his mom called it.

Gross.

He wasn't a puppy, and he wasn't in love.

Heli wasn't on the back porch. She'd left the light on especially for him. He could see her in the kitchen through the back door, covered in flour and popping chocolate chips like they were Prozac. Even from here he could smell her delicious scent. Butter and brown sugar, sure, but also something sweet and ripe, like plums.

God, he had to quit thinking like a damn fool in love. He was here to break up with sexy, sensual, delicious Heli. He should remember that. He'd tried once before and hadn't been able to stay away. She'd taken him back with a little cajoling and a whole lot of orgasms. If he was going to get her out of his system and make her believe this was the end for real this time, he really had to sell it.

He had to be the worst kind of asshole. The love 'em and leave 'em kind.

HELI'S HELL

The two things holding Heli's head above drowning in fear and depression were chocolate chips and orgasms. Without either, she'd probably be a big snot-bubble mess sitting in the corner crying. She simply wasn't emotionally equipped to deal with her sister being kidnapped, her best friend becoming a werewolf, and the local grocery store refusing to stock the imported French butter that made all of her baked goods taste like heaven.

Her life, up until a few weeks ago, had been easy peasy lemon squeezy cheezy. Her parents were still happily married, she'd recently graduated from culinary school with flying colors, and the hot guy she'd never thought would look twice at a big-bottomed girl like her, had finally made a move. She shouldn't be freaking out... she even had anxiety about having all these feelings. Blurgh.

Most things in life came like a piece of cake for her. No

trauma, no drama, and she was happy as a llama in PJs. Until the wolves came.

Nope, she couldn't handle it. Which was why she was up at two o'clock in the morning making her third trial batch of maple bacon oatmeal chocolate chip cookies. That and waiting for Kosta to come over. Because while the sugar rush gave her brain all the sparklies of a cocaine addict, nothing helped her sleep like snuggling into Kosta's big strong arms after a long bout of orgasmic fun.

Tonight was a big deal for the Troikas, and she knew he was going to be busy. Gal had invited Heli to come to the mating ceremony, but it wasn't like a wedding or anything. The couples were gonna have sex, in front of everyone. She didn't need to see that. Especially the part where afterwards they'd all turn into wolves and go trouncing around the Reserve.

It was already weird enough that every other person in her life was actually a werewolf, including Kosta. At least they weren't mafia like she'd thought before Max had revealed their true natures to Gal. That had been one hell of a night. She could deal with the fact that the supernatural existed. Fine, whatever. It actually explained a lot.

What pissed her off was that they should all be out helping her find Zara. No one had any doubt that one of the packs the wolves in Rogue were at war with were to blame. All because her sister was Niko Troika's ex-girlfriend. So no, she didn't want to go to their little full-moon orgy.

Her beautiful, strong, smart, lovely older sister could be

dead or worse. Heli shoved a spoonful of cookie dough into her mouth. That helped. No going into freak out mode.

Heli smashed her knuckles into a burnt cookie. Niko, the butthead, had not only broken Zara's heart, he'd gone off and assassinated the president of all the wolves or something.

Heli wanted to go out and look for clues, ask questions, maybe even try to infiltrate another pack. She had no idea what she was even talking about. But that's what people did in the cozy mystery and romantic suspense novels she liked to read. It wasn't like she had any real-world experience with kidnapping and murder.

The vile taste of bile bubbled in the back of her throat and she popped another handful of chocolate chips in her mouth to combat it. She wished Kosta would get here soon.

Then there he was, an enormous but beautiful black wolf, sitting under the soft glow of the porch light, staring at her though the screen like she was the most tempting of little red riding hoods. Every time she saw him like this, it took her breath away and made her heart go ka-thump.

"I wasn't sure you'd come tonight." She pushed the door open to let him inside.

I couldn't stay away. You've been on my mind all night, zaika.

His voice was low and growly when he was in his wolf form and it did exciting things to her girly bits. She wasn't quite used to him talking in her head like that, but she didn't dislike it. Knowing she was the only one who could hear him when he did that had a very intimate feel to it.

Plus, she loved flirting with him. "You just followed the scent of cookies to my door. I see how you are."

I can scent your desire far beyond the reach of your cookies. They aren't nearly as delicious to me as your pussy.

"Aw, you say the sweetest things." She not-so-secretly loved when he talked dirty like that. Already she felt a thousand times better than she had even five minutes and seven cookies ago. If she wasn't careful, she was going to get addicted to him instead of chocolate.

His wolfy eyes twinkled and he slowly stalked around the kitchen island to get to her. *You're the sweetest thing. Come over here and let me taste you.*

Heli scooted to the other side of the counter and pointed a finger first at him and then the timer counting down. "You're naughty. You have to wait until the batch in the oven comes out. I already burned these, and I promised to bring some to Galyna's library meeting tomorrow. She's bribing the assistant manager with them, so he'll cover her shifts for a few days."

Kosta looked at the slightly darkened cookies on the counter, swiped up four or five with his big floppy canine tongue and chewed them while staring her down. Then he used his nose to boop the off button on the oven. *There, problem solved.*

Gasp. One did not simply turn the oven off in the middle of making cookies. "Hey. Now this batch will be underdone, and I don't have anything to show for my night."

The wolf reared its head back and with some cracking and popping and some shedding of fur, a naked man stood in its place. So naked. So, so gloriously well hung. Kosta grabbed his dick, that she'd been blatantly staring at, and gave it a couple of long strokes. "I've got something to show you for your night."

Her brain screeched to a halt and her flirtability went from on fire to burned up and in the garbage in a flash. Seeing him naked, with those six-thousand pack abs, that vee of muscles at his hips that should be illegal, and his cock all hard for her... wait what was she saying? "Yeah. Show me."

She expected some other quip from him, but he took two fast strides toward her, picked her up like a friggin fairy princess and marched her down the hall to her bedroom. He dropped her onto her bed and whipped her nightgown up and over her head faster than you can say chocolate chip cookies.

"I can also scent your tears from earlier, Heli. I wish there was a way I could make you less distressed about Zara. Besides making you come." He gently pushed her back and wedged a knee between her bare thighs. "I've already promised to tell you the second we hear anything."

Heli grabbed his shoulders and pulled him down to her, wanting his warmth, wanting him to make her forget everything but how good it felt to be with him. Except he'd mentioned Zara and now her brain was flooding with anxiety. "I know you have. I was hoping tomorrow we might go out and actually look for her ourselves. I hate sitting around having nothing to do but worry. Please, will you help me find her?"

Kosta sighed and pressed his forehead to hers. "Hel, it's too dangerous for you to go out actively looking for Zara. You've only seen a taste of what a pack war can be like. Especially with the Troikas on so many other wolves' shit lists. One whiff of me on your soft, sweet skin and you'd become a target too. I can't allow that to happen."

Dammit. She knew they shouldn't have started talking about this. She scooted away from him and grabbed a pillow, clutching it in front of her body as she leaned against the headboard. What was she supposed to say to that? Fine? It wasn't fine. She got that he wanted to keep her safe, but he had to see she couldn't do nothing anymore.

"Sweetheart, I can scent your anger. Don't be mad." Kosta sat back on his knees and scratched his balls.

"Seriously? I shouldn't be upset? My sister has been missing for weeks. I'm lying to my parents about it so I don't expose you and your pack to more humans, and I'm just supposed to be happy and cheery? I'm not some Stepford plus-sized Barbie. I'm human. Maybe wolf girls just let you be all alpha-in-charge and do whatever you say, but I'm not a wolf."

His eyes narrowed and he stilled. "No. I haven't forgotten for even a second that you're not one of my kind."

Whoa. The way he said that had her feeling like she was less than him. He'd never made her feel that way before, not even before she knew he wasn't human. He was super-fit, she was plump, and the only running she did was to the grocery store. That hadn't ever mattered. While she knew she was cute and had great boobs, she wasn't a ten. He was smoking and was like an eleventy-hundred on the hotness scale. Kosta hadn't seemed to notice.

There were lots of disparities between them and never, ever had he acted superior, until right now. Did he actually believe wolf-shifters were a superior race? Gal had said part of the politics behind this war was about that exact issue.

"Is that a problem? It never was before."

"Things have changed." He looked down, around, anywhere but at her.

All that warmth she'd felt when he showed up was gone, turned to ice cubes.

"Holy cakeballs. Are you breaking up with me? What was this? Trying to get some before you got cut off?" She waved her hand up and down her hidden naked body.

Kosta got up and looked around the floor for his pants. "No."

Gah. He was so lying.

Heli threw the pillow at him, got up, shoved her feet in her favorite bunny slippers and grabbed her robe off the back of the closet door. "A. You didn't flipping bring pants, and two, don't lie to me. You were. You thought we were gonna have break up sex."

Kosta held out his hands, palms up like he was Jesus or something. "Heli."

"Don't Heli me. I thought we meant a little bit more to each other than that. Don't get that oh-no she's a crazy girl who thinks we're in love, gonna get married, and have babies freaked out look on your face. I'm not in love with you, but I seriously like you a lot. You made me feel not so scared and alone when Zara went missing." Now she was questioning everything. Whether he actually liked her or not, whether she was just another in a long string of notches on his belt.

With every one of those thoughts she got angrier, mostly at herself for not seeing through his charm and charisma. She wrapped her robe around waist and tied it tight. The guy owned a strip club for goodness sake, that was not husband or even boyfriend material.

A huge lump formed right in the middle of her throat. That was not a conscious thought she'd given any time to ponder before. She wasn't looking for a husband. He wasn't looking for a mate. They weren't even a good match anyway. Heli had to swallow a few times to get that last lie to herself down.

Dammit. She marched toward the kitchen, Kosta hot on her heels, and yanked open the still warm oven. The cookies inside were done perfectly. Figures. She grabbed one and threw it at his head.

Kosta snagged the cookie out of the air with those faster than human reflexes. "I'm sorry. It's not you, Hel."

"Oh. My. God." She threw another cookie at him, this

time aiming lower. "Do not even for one second say it's not you, it's me."

He turned and the cookie smacked him on the hip. That wouldn't even leave a bruise. "I have to be with my own kind for a while. This pack war thing is more dangerous than you could ever understand."

What a bastard. No way she was wasting another bit of her tenderness or delicious baked goods on him. Burnt ones on the other hand made for better weapons. She grabbed the biggest cookie on the countertop and pointed it at him. "Fine. Go. Be with your own kind. I'll go find Zara on my own."

"No, you will not." He snagged her weapon and crushed it into a thousand tiny pieces that crumbled out of his hand and to the floor.

Heli put her hands on her hips and glared at the destroyer of cookies and hearts. "Watch me."

Kosta grabbed her around the waist and pulled her tight against his hard body. "Heli. Do not put yourself in danger that way. Promise me you won't."

There was something new in his voice, a tone or an intonation that resonated deep within her. She wanted badly to do what he said. She fought off that urge. "I'm not making any promises to you."

"Dammit, *zaika.* Everything in my life is already going to shit, if you were to get hurt in a war you shouldn't even be involved in, I'd have to burn down the world." The brilliance of his blue eyes swirled with a darker, almost purple color and she could see the wolf in him rising to the surface.

Another retort was right on the tip of her tongue, but her brained clicked in to what he'd just said. He'd burn down the world... for her. She wasn't as dumb as she thought. He did have feelings for her. Big ones. He was pushing her away on purpose, out of some sort of idea that she'd be safer if they weren't together.

Aww.

Okay, now they were going to have break-up sex. Then make up sex.

Kosta cupped her chin and cheek in one of his big strong hands. "If I promise to search for Zara on my own will you be satisfied?"

Not really, but he was trying. More than anyone else. "Let me help. I know her the best."

"I know you do," he brushed his thumb across her lips, "and if you were a wolftress, I'd have you by my side in a second. But you humans are so fragile. I can't take that kind of chance with you. Not for anything."

But she wasn't. She wasn't anything extraordinary. A simple girl who loved her family, mystery novels, chocolate, and had a crush on a guy way too hot for her. A really good guy, who was something special. "You're going to put yourself in danger though, aren't you. That's why you came here tonight to break up with me."

Those swirls in his eyes went even darker. His gaze flicked down to her lips and back. "This would all be a lot easier if you'd let me."

"Do it then." Heli stood up on her tippy toes and slid her

lips across his. She whispered against his mouth. "Say the words, then. Break up with me and I'll let you go so you can do what you need to."

"*Zaika*," he groaned. "That's not exactly how this was supposed to work. You have to be mad at me, throw me out, and tell me never to come back."

Heli pushed her hands into his hair and pulled him down. She tipped her head to the side and Kosta licked and nibbled the sensitive skin at her throat. His mouth there always sent a rush of tingles through her body. "I do want you to come back."

Kosta growled deep in his chest in that insanely sexy way that turned her on. He lifted her up and set her butt on the countertop, pushing his way between her legs. "I want you to come for me. One last time."

He was so tall that they were already aligned and he would only have to thrust his hips forward to push his way inside of her. She wanted that more than anything. If he really was leaving to go find Zara or something in this crazy pack war, she didn't know when she'd see him again.

Instead of taking her there on the kitchen counter, Kosta dropped to one knee and pushed that sexy bearded face between her thighs. "Come for me, my little bunny."

She was already riled up from their almost sex before, plus their fight had gotten her blood flowing too. It wasn't going to take much more than a lick in just the right place to get her to climax. Kosta did so much more than that. The man was an artist with his tongue and a master with his teeth.

He scraped his beard along her inner thighs in the way that drove her crazy and followed that burn with his wet tongue.

Heli shivered. “Don’t tease me, Kosta. Please.”

“Careful what you wish for.” He wrapped his lips around her clit and sucked hard. Her hips came up off the counter, but he pushed her back down, wrapping his arms around her legs. He hummed his disapproval of her. The tiny vibrations felt oh, so good.

Heli pushed her hands into his hair and gripped the strands tight, wishing this was enough to hold him close for more than just the night. “Please, Kosta. Yes, yes.”

Kosta responded to her pleas by filling her with two fingers and tap, tap, tapped in just the right spot. His tongue lashed at her in all the best ways and her orgasm struck with the power of a seven point one earthquake. She cried out his name and her legs reflexively tried to close, which made Kosta hold her open even more.

He stood and pressed his thumb onto her pulsating clit and dragged his fingers right over her g-spot. "Give me another one, Heli."

"God, Kosta." There was something desperate in his need now and it spiked hers too. Her inner muscles clenched around his fingers, wanting more. "Fuck me, now."

"Give this to me first, I need to know this cunt is only for me. That you come only for me." His naughty words had that new sexy intonation that did something to her will-power making it impossible to refuse him anything.

Not that she wanted to say no. The tension inside of her was building, building, building toward a second luscious climax. The pressure on her already sensitive clit from his thumb and the way he filled her was the perfect storm of pleasure. He knew her body better than any other lover, sometimes better than she knew herself. Throw in those wolf eyes of his glowing like never before and his canine fangs descending, and she was lost to him. He was wild and damn sexy all riled up like this, so raw and animalistic. "Yes, Kosta. Only for you."

He gave her a pleased growl and pushed a third finger inside of her. "That's right. Now let me see you come, you're so fucking beautiful when you come for me."

It was the way he said those words more than anything else that pushed her over the edge into that second orgasm. Her body clenched around Kosta's fingers so hard that even her stomach muscles bunched up, and for a second she couldn't breathe. Then Kosta's mouth was back at her neck, scraping his teeth across her skin and the wave of pure bliss hit her, taking her body and mind into the warm rush of afterglow.

He whispered in her ear. "Goodbye, *zaika*."

Kosta stepped away, shifted back into the beautiful black wolf, and then he was gone.

He was gone.

ALWAYS LISTEN TO YOUR WOLF

Kosta should have gone straight to his car after leaving Heli like the asshole he was. Instead, he let his wolf take over and run free through the Reserve until sunrise. His animal side had tried several times to point him back in the direction of Heli's house. Kosta had pushed on, finding prey to hunt and distract himself from all thoughts of her.

That strategy did distract his wolf, but his human mind was overthinking the fuck out of what happened and what he was going to do about it.

He shouldn't have let Heli see his feelings for her. Dammit, he didn't even want to have feelings for her. They were going to get in the way. He needed to have one focus and that was to infiltrate and take down the Bay pack from the inside. To do that he needed to make everyone he loved think he was the worst. Worst boyfriend, worst brother, worst son.

Heli was probably pissed right now that he'd left her laying on her kitchen counter. He had to get out of there. He'd been this close to marking her with his bite. No way was he prepared to even think about what that meant. Nope. He was not biting a human. Even if his wolf was begging him to.

His mouth watered thinking about the rush of the moment, having her admit that she was his. He hadn't even meant to push her to say that. His wolf had been so close to the surface, having her spread out, open and submitting to his will. Those were the thoughts of an alpha, not him. His wolf didn't care, it wanted to be in charge, even if that wasn't his destiny.

That was probably exactly how his brother had ended up mated to Gal. There was still a part of Kosta that was angry at Max for taking over the pack from Niko. The two of them were never supposed to be alphas and had formed their own sort of bond over that. But it was hard to fault him for falling in love with Galyna. She was cool as shit and perfect for Max.

Kosta chased a fat little brown bunny, thinking it would make a nice snack. His heart wasn't in it though. He'd lost his taste for them. Might as well head back to his car. If he was leaving Troika territory for a while, he needed to make sure the club was taken care of before he left and that meant a shit ton of paperwork and payroll to get prepped.

He stopped by the tree he'd left his clothes in, shifted, and got dressed. He checked his phone, not wanting to admit he hoped for missed calls from her. Nope, not one.

Good, that was for the best. He did have one text from an unknown number.

Arrangements are being made. We'll be in contact soon.

Kosta rolled his eyes at their attempt at subterfuge. He shoved his phone in his pocket and jogged toward the edge of the Reserve.

The rest of the cars were gone from the parking lot, but someone else was here. He caught her scent before he saw her. Dog gone it. Heli was sitting in the passenger seat of his truck. He really ought to have locked it. Dumbass.

He walked up to her side, tapped on the window making her jump, and crossed his arms.

Heli cranked the old-style handle and rolled the glass down. "Good try, asshole. That was a real dick move, leaving me like that, but I see through you now. I believed it the first time, even cried my eyes out and ate way too much peanut butter chocolate chip ice cream over you. We are not breaking up and that's final."

Kosta rubbed his forehead. What was he going to do with her? "Heli. Get out of my truck."

She huffed and folded her arms. "No. You said you're going to look for Zara. I'm coming with."

This would be a whole lot easier if she wasn't so fucking cute, sitting there in what he was sure she deemed spy clothes. She was in all black, with a leather jacket and knee high boots. With her ass, those black leggings were lethal. "It's too dangerous."

Heli tilted her head up and peeked at him through those

long lashes, batting them at him. She smiled and he was dead. "You'll protect me."

But who was going to protect him from her? Kosta gave up for the moment and crossed to the driver's side. He unlocked his door with the key. Hey, wait a minute, he had locked the truck. "How did you get in here?"

Heli showed him her phone and pointed to a bag at her feet with a wire coat hanger sticking out of it. "I googled how to break in. There was a very helpful video on YouTube."

It was a little ridiculous how proud of her he was at this precise moment. Smart and a touch of bad girl made her extra hot. Wait, no. He was supposed to be pushing her away. What he really wanted to do was pull her across the bench seat and into his lap. What he was going to do was drive her home. He started the truck and put it in gear.

"Where are we going? Do you have a lead on who took Zara? Do tasers work on werewolves?" She pulled out a hot pink tube, about five inches long and showed it to him.

He'd never been tased, but he didn't see why not. What she held in her hand was not a taser though. It didn't look that much bigger than a tube of lipstick. Or a vibrator. "What is that?"

She dangled the contraption from a key chain. "It's my taser pepper spray flashlight baton."

On one hand he was glad she carried some kind of self defense in her bag. On the other, he wanted to howl and growl that she might ever need anything like it. He should be there to protect her at all costs. "Where did you get that?"

"Amazon."

Lord save him from online shopping. "I don't think that's going to stop a wolf who's coming at your throat, doll."

"Oh, well, good thing I've got you then." She shoved the piece of crap back in her bag and tapped on the dash. "Let's hit the road, Jack. Times a wastin'."

Shit. "Heli. I'm taking you home. You can not go where I'm headed. We talked about this."

"You talked, I never agreed. I'm not going anywhere that isn't toward finding Zara. I guess I could go out on my own. Gal said there's another pack nearby that Max is worried about. I'll start there." She moved to open her door like she was going to get out.

He needed a distraction and quick. He considered for one second kissing her senseless, but it wouldn't do him any good. She was too smart and would probably figure out what he was trying to do, and even if she didn't, they'd be right back where they started. Except he'd be hard as stone again. No, he needed a different strategy if he was going to keep her safe and her nose out of pack business.

Who did he know that was sneaky like a fox and would help him out? He could only think of one person. His mother.

"Fine. I can see that you're determined. Let's go."

Heli bounced on her seat like an excited kid and then buckled her seat belt. "I'm ready."

The drive to the pack house was short. His mother kept a room there for each of them, but he had his own apartment over the club. His own little sanctuary away from everyone else. He kept that locked up good and tight. No one was allowed upstairs, man nor beast.

"What are we doing here?"

"You don't think I'm going off to save Zara on my own. Packs don't work that way, that's why it's called a pack and not a lone." It was one more reason the rest of the Troikas wouldn't suspect he was going in to sabotage the Bays. Lone wolves were generally not good people. Either they'd left or been kicked out of their packs, banished for crimes against wolfkind, or they were psychopaths who thrived without society breathing down their necks.

Some lone wolves found other packs. Some founded them.

Kosta was going to have to convince the Bays he'd gone lone and left his pack. First he was going to have to convince his pack he'd left. Picking a fight with Heli had shown him that wasn't going to work. His mother would see through that ruse too. He'd have to give them both some sort of variation of the truth, something he believed enough so his mother and brothers wouldn't scent the lie.

They entered through the kitchen door because he smelled bacon and eggs and knew his mom was up making breakfast. For a wolf, she didn't keep their late hours. Never had. "Mom? Got some breakfast for us?"

Selena stood at the kitchen sink in a thousand dollar

outfit and a 1950's apron. "Of course, *sinochek*. Come in, sit down."

She set a plate of eggs and bacon exactly the way he liked it, barely crisp, in front of Kosta. He shoveled the food in with no preamble. Fucking Heli and then running around the reserve had given him a serious appetite.

"Heli, fresh baked scones for you, dear. Cinnamon or blueberry?"

"Oh, gosh, thanks. I thought I was gonna have to gag down eggs and undercooked bacon." She covered her mouth and her eyes went wide. "Sorry. I didn't mean that your cooking is in any way bad. I–"

His mother set one of each kind of scone in front of Heli and a couple in front of him. "Don't be silly. I knew you were mostly vegetarian. I've expanded my repertoire for meatless dishes quite a bit since you and Kosta, ahem, got together."

How in the hell did his mother know she was vegetarian and he didn't? She'd been keeping tabs on Heli, that's how. She'd better not be trying to match make. He scraped the last of the eggs into his mouth, and stole one more piece of bacon from his mother's plate. He washed it all down with the big glass of orange juice she set in front of him. "So, uh, bad or good news, depending on how you see it, mom. Heli has figured out our plans to rescue Zara.

Selena narrowed her eyes at her son, picked up a scone, buttered it and shoved it at him, but she also didn't miss a beat and played along. "Did she now? What do you want to do about that?"

"I was hoping you might fill her in and see what she could do to help the effort while I go do some recon with Max today." He made eyes at her that he hoped she interpreted as *please help keep Heli safe and get her off the idea that she can go out into other packs' territories*. That was a lot to shove into one look, but his mom was a pro. If he didn't know better, he'd have guessed she was a little bit psychic even.

Heli took a bite of her scone and made mean eyes at him. She was already suspicious. Screw. The longer he sat here with the two of them, the deeper into trouble he was going to get. He stood up quickly, shoving his chair back until it almost toppled over. "You don't mind if I take a quick shower and grab some clothes, do you, mom?"

He scooted around the table and toward the doorway, stopping on the way to give Heli a quick kiss on the shoulder. "You two talk. I won't be long."

That last part wasn't really a lie. It wouldn't take a moment to grab those clothes and sneak out the window of his old room. Both women were going to kick his ass the next time they saw him. He just hoped that he would actually get to see them again.

He riffled through the closet, found a couple of changes of clothes, so he wouldn't have to do laundry at least for another day, and snuck out in the same way he had in high school, except this time it was in broad daylight. His truck would make too much noise, so he jogged through the neighborhood and toward the edge of the business district. Rogue was a small enough town that it only took him about twenty minutes to get to his apartment anyway.

As he approached the corner where his business was located, he heard the boom boom boom of the club's music coming from the main floor. It was a little early in the morning for strippers' hours. He crept in and found a whole room full of women dancing and giggling and getting their groove thangs on. Helena, also known as Sinnamon Twist, waved from the stage.

"Everybody say hey to our lovely host, Kosta." She waved and then spun around her pole.

All eyes turned on him. There went any chance of being incognito. He waved and winked at one of the girls in the back row. All the women here were dressed in workout clothes and flushed from exercise. He'd forgotten about Saturday morning pole dance class. It had been the dancers' idea. Since the club wasn't open in the mornings, they wanted to use the floor to teach exercise classes.

Worked for him, since it brought in more money and new clientele. Especially for ladies night. Women who'd been to the club to workout were less intimidated about coming for a male review. Speaking of which, he needed to find some new talent.

"Ladies, practice those back hook spins for a minute, I'll be right back." Helena jumped down from the stage and trotted over to him. "Hey, bossman. There's a couple of dudes waiting for you in your office. They really didn't like when I told them they couldn't watch class."

"Sorry about that, doll. I'll take care of them. You do

your thing."

She saluted and went back to her class. Kosta didn't allow anyone to make his girls feel uncomfortable. Yeah this was a strip club, but it was a classy one. The talent was just that, extremely talented dancers who liked making lots of extra money putting on a show. He was always careful about who he hired and who he let into the club. He did not like that someone unsavory got in without him being there.

He was going to have to hire a couple more bouncers to add into the rotation so they could cover weekend morning pole classes too, especially if he wasn't going to be here himself. Maybe Aleksei. That guy needed something to do besides blame himself for the death of their Alpha. Another line on his growing to-do list.

Kosta made his way to his office and opened up his senses to figure out who the dickheads waiting for him might be. It took less than a second. Salty, briny, stank. Bay pack enforcers, but not the same ones from last night.

Sending these two to his place of business in the smack dead center of Troika territory was a power play by their alpha, Decker.

No time like the present to let Bay know he wasn't one to be bullied and his club was off limits. Kosta peeked around the corner and saw the two enforcers lounging in the comfy visitor chairs he had at his desk. They were in enemy territory and weren't even on their guard. Dumb. As long as the Bay enforcers kept making stupid mistakes, he'd keep teaching them lessons in security. Maybe Decker was recruiting him because he knew he was surrounded by incompetence.

Kosta crept into the office quietly and grabbed both by the scruff of their necks, which in human form was damn uncomfortable. "What the hell are you two doing in Troika territory?"

The bigger of the two wriggled and tried to slap at Kosta's hands. "Hey man, Decker sent us. No need for your little show. We know whose side you're on and there ain't no one else around to worry about hearing us."

Typical one-blood mentality. There was an entire room full of human women and they didn't think, even for a minute, that any mattered, much less that any of the girls might hear what they were saying and cause a problem. He didn't like anything about them or their pack.

They didn't need to know that. If they thought he was putting up a front he'd play along. He let them go, not so gently, and both tumbled back onto the ground. "You never know who is watching or listening. A good enforcer needs to keep that in mind."

The smaller guy threw his thumb over his shoulder. "Those chicks out there are–"

Kosta leaned against the edge of his desk and folded his arms. In a dark, low tone he interrupted. "I'd suggest you not finish that sentence, unless you want my fist in your mouth. Like I said, you never know."

The two enforcers exchanged looks. They definitely weren't used to keeping themselves in check around humans, that much he could see. Things over in the Bay must be worse than he thought. He and the rest of the Troikas had been so tied up in fighting off the Grimm and Crescent packs after their father had been killed, they hadn't checked in with others in the area . No way Max could do that now. This little meeting just confirmed that Kosta was doing the right thing.

"What do you want?" He might as well get the ball rolling for them.

"Deck..., uh, someone you know," the wolf looked over his shoulder like now he was concerned about who was listening, "wants to, uh, invest in your business. If you know what I mean."

What a douche. "Keep talking."

"He's been keeping an eye on you, and likes what you've got here. Thinks your biz could work good with his. There are, uh, more places that could use women with the kind of skills your ladies happen to have."

So that's why Decker was interested in him. Not because he needed better enforcers. No, he wanted to exploit the strip club. Well, fuck that shit. "My ladies aren't for sale."

The smaller guy took his turn at cajoling Kosta. Decker had sent him a couple of used car salesmen. "We get it. You want to keep them all to yourself. Deck, I mean, our boss, thought you might feel that way. He wants you to know that with his plans, you'll have more pussy than you'll know what to do with."

That did not bode well. There was no doubt in Kosta's mind that he wasn't talking about wolftresses. That meant they were exploiting human women like the Grimms had started to do before Max and Gal had put a stop to it. This was much more serious than he'd imagined. Were they also biting these women? There could be a whole harem of marked women running around with psychic powers or brand new shifter abilities.

Maybe he should bring Max in on this. He needed a lot more details before he would think about asking for help. "Where exactly is he getting all this pussy?"

The smaller guy got a smug look on his face. "That's for us to know, and you to find out when he comes to your little den of iniquity to visit tonight."

Yeah, no. He didn't want Decker or his entourage anywhere near the Naughty Wolf. "I'm busy tonight. It's Saturday and I've got a business to run."

"The boss's offer is take it or leave it. You don't want to make an enemy of the Bay pack, Troika."

Sure he did. He needed in, but without letting them make him into some kind of beta lackey. "Fine. I will meet with Decker. But on my terms."

"We'll see about that. Decker doesn't like upstarts." These two wouldn't know an upstart if it hit them in the face.

Kosta had a lot of work to do in the next eighteen hours. He had to turn over the running of the club to his assistant manager, steer clear of Heli all day, and make his family think he'd betrayed them all. "I'll be at the Bay pack house around midnight. Decker can show me what he's offering then."

DUMB BLONDES AND OTHER SMART WOMEN

Heli wasn't dumb. She knew Kosta had just ghosted her and his mom. She calmly buttered a second scone, because they were damn good, and smiled at Selena. "Kosta is trying to protect me. I get that, but I hope you understand that I can't sit around and wait for someone else to rescue my sister."

Selena sipped her coffee and nodded. "I would expect no less from you. You wouldn't be in my Konstantin's life if you were the kind of girl who couldn't take care of herself, and those she cared about."

Umm. That wasn't what she expected. Heli didn't think Selena would be on the level with her. Bonus. "I have a sense he's planning on doing something dangerous."

"Mmm-hmm. I'm sure he is. Out to prove himself. It's the curse of being the youngest boy in the family, I'm afraid." Selena didn't seem very concerned. Must come from raising three boys who were also wolves.

"Can I ask you something?" If Selena was going to be real with her, Heli was going to get to the core of what she cared about.

"Of course. Anything, *lapachka*." Selena picked up another piece of bacon and munched on it. She looked directly at Heli, but her eyes flitted around like she was thinking about something else entirely.

Selena clearly had other stuff to do besides babysit Heli. She was sort of the queen mother to the pack. Might as well get right to the point, so both of them could do what they needed to. "Is there really a plan to find Zara?"

Selena placed her hand on Heli's and squeezed gently, her full attention on her. "Heli, you and your sister are very important to me and my family, even if neither of you understands it yet. I swear to you, I have people working on keeping Zara safe. We will do everything in our power to bring her home."

The rock that had been sitting on Heli's chest for days crumbled a little and became a smidge lighter. Keeping her safe. That implied that Selena knew where Zara was. "Can't we bring her home now?"

"A revolution doesn't happen overnight."

Galyna had explained some of what was going on with the whole pack politics stuff. How the wolves hadn't been allowed to choose their own mates or something. Selena had been working to change all that.

It was great and all, but she didn't like that Zara's life was in jeopardy for the cause. The two of them hadn't even known about werewolves until like a week ago. They shouldn't have to be casualties of someone else's war. Heli just wanted her sister back. "No, but a rescue mission could."

"Yes, you are correct, but I don't have all the right people in place to rescue Zara." That blue glow that meant her wolf was close to the surface lit up Selena's eyes. "If we don't do it right, lives will be destroyed."

Heli wasn't sure if that was a warning or a premonition. Either way she didn't like it. "You know something you aren't telling me."

"Yes." The glow brightened and the distracted look was back. It was more than distracted. Selena was worried, and it was bringing her wolf out.

Heli was being an ass. She hadn't been thinking about anyone but herself and hadn't noticed the dark smudges around Selena's eyes that came with lack of sleep. There were new creases across her forehead and around her mouth too. The outfit she wore was still high end and really nice but the usual accessories were gone. Maybe this pack war was harder on a mother than Heli had considered. Her first born, Niko, was already half lost because of it. "Could you tell me?"

"No." She gave a half-shrug. "It won't help you find Zara, if that is what you're going to do. I can't help you put yourself in danger that way."

Selena was an ally, but she was as bad as Kosta. Worse because she was a mother. Heli was back to knowing she was going to have to go out and search for Zara on her own, which was going to be more dangerous than if they'd helped her in the first place. It sure would have been nice to have some wolves with their noses and special supernatural senses.

Screw that. She was still going to use a wolf to help her. He just couldn't find out until it was too late. Kosta would be mad, but she'd take a mad boyfriend over a missing sister every day, all day, twice on Sundays.

"Heli." Selena said her name in that chastising way all moms had when they knew you were up to something.

"Oh, sorry. Daydreaming." Sort of.

Selena smiled at her, but then must have heard a noise Heli couldn't. She turned her head and listened, then set her cup down. "Plotting more like."

Busted.

"I'm, umm, gonna go." Before Selena sniffed out what Heli was really thinking and tried to stop her.

"I need to take care of some things too." She glanced out the kitchen's archway. "There's a small package for you by the door. Take it and be careful. Use your gifts."

Gifts? The ability to make melt in your mouth chocolate cream puffs probably wasn't going to help her find Zara.

Something thumped against the wall in the hallway where the bedrooms were located in the big house, followed by two or three more thumps and the sound of wood cracking. If she had to guess, it sounded like someone was punching the wall or a door hard enough to bust the wood. "Is everything alright?"

"Not yet." Selena stood and glanced in the direction the

sounds were coming from with a whole lot of worry and blue glow in her eyes. "Off you go now. Take care of Kosta. He hasn't figured out he needs someone who will both challenge and take care of him yet. He will, don't lose faith in that."

Selena pointed to the front door, where there was indeed a small brown paper package with her name on it. Then she hurried toward the bedrooms. An angry, low growl echoed in the hallway that made Heli speed up her pace out of the house. She paused only for a second to grab the package lying next to a pile of some kind of fancy tea party invitations and Kosta's keys from the little table next to the door. She bolted out and took the steps two at a time. She was back in Kosta's truck in a hurry.

It took her a minute to figure out how to move the seat forward so she could reach the pedals. Kosta was a whole lot taller and had way longer legs than her. Heli finally found the latch, but it was a pain to move that whole bench forward. The steering wheel was practically in her lap now. She felt like the little old lady from Pasadena driving this big honking thing.

As she pulled out of the long driveway of the Troika house, she caught a glimpse out of the corner of her eye of a naked man running toward the woods. Damn. Not just any naked man. Niko.

A pretty caramel colored wolf ran after him. That must be Selena.

Cripes. Heli felt awful for keeping Selena all that time when it was clear she needed to be taking care of Niko.

What if Heli did get Zara back and she came home to find the love of her life had gone bat-shit crazy?

They would have to cross that bridge when they got to it. Heli had to find Zara first. After she pulled up to her house and parked Kosta's truck in the drive, she pulled out her phone and texted Helena. She didn't like asking her friend to be a spy, but it wouldn't hurt just to ask if she'd seen him.

Finding Kosta was still step one in her plan. This time she needed him not to know she was following him. That would be hard to do with his sense of smell, but she had an idea for that too.

Hey, sorry I missed pole class this morning. Had a bit of a fight with K. Did you see him?

There. That sounded natural.

Yeah. He was here with some freaky guys.

Freaky guys? Helena saw all kinds in her line of work, so for her to think someone was alarming spoke volumes.

She tapped back hoping for details. This could be a clue, because Heli would bet that creepy vibe Helena got was a predator, also known as the bad guy wolves. *Are they still there?*

Helena's reply seemed to take an eternity. *Nope. Left a couple of mins ago. Thank goodness. K's still here. You coming over?*

Damn, no baddies to tail. At least she knew where Kosta was. She could drive over to Sleepy Folk and park his truck there. It was going to be hard to follow him anywhere if he didn't have a car. But even if he had some kind of backup transportation, which he must if he just ditched his car at his mom's, she wouldn't be very stealthy following him around in a purple 1950's classic pickup truck. Either way, she wasn't driving it, which meant she was walking since she didn't own a car. Maybe there was an Uber Spy she could use. Wasn't that in a movie?

She decided to leave the truck at her house and hoof it into town. She planted the opposite idea and if she was lucky Helena would tell Kosta. *IDK. I think I'll stay home and let him come to me after he's cooled down.*

Her reply came back right away. *Need me to rip him a new one?*

It was nice to know she had friends who would kick her boyfriend's behind if and when he needed it. *lol - no. He just didn't want to do something I wanted to and it turned into a whole thing. It's fine.*

Are we talking sex positions here?

Heli could practically hear Helena's voice going up an octave with excitement.

OMG. NO. He was just being a butt. A cute butt, that wanted to keep her safe. She did love him for wanting to protect her. She'd love him more if he'd realize she didn't need protecting, but help.

Wait. You guys are doing butt stuff now?

Heli rolled her eyes and laughed. *You have a one track mind. I'm going now.*

Helena sent back a winky face.

The new plan was forming in her mind little by little. She knew without a doubt that Kosta was going on some secret mission. It was almost as if she could see him doing all these dumb things in her mind.

She didn't know if it was to find Zara or not, but even if it wasn't, wherever he was going, if there were other wolf packs involved, there would be clues. A pack had abducted a human woman. That had to be big news or at least rumors about it. Heli planned to be around to hear them.

First stop, the hunting supply store, but not for a gun. She wasn't sure she could ever shoot anyone. No, what she needed was a way to disguise her scent. She'd heard that hunters used deer urine. Sounded super disgusting, but Kosta had demonstrated over and over again that wolves could smell everything. Like everything.

Maybe if she smelled like deer pee he wouldn't know it was her, just think she was an incontinent forest animal.

She slid out of the truck and the package that Selena had given her thunked to the ground. She picked it up and tore open the brown paper. There was a small glass perfume spritzer with a note wrapped around it.

You smell like your wolf. This might come in handy.

Rude. Heli's cheeks and throat went all hot. Wait. Not you smell like a wolf, but your wolf. At least Kosta's mom shipped them. Heli popped off the lid and spritzed a little into it. She waved it around and then smelled the cap. Nothing. She gave it another squirt. Still nothing. Weird. Even water smelled like something.

Heli sniffed her arm where she'd put on her warm vanilla and brown sugar lotion this morning. Yeah, that she could smell. She squirted a little of the mystery scent on her arm and sniffed it again.

Whoa, she couldn't smell the lotion.

Bad ass. Now she didn't have to stop for deer pee, or smell like it. That gave her time to eat and pack a snack for later. She had no idea how long she was going to be following and watching Kosta. The stake outs in the books and movies never seemed to last that long, but inevitably someone got hungry and went out for food and missed what they were looking for.

She made a quick hummus and roasted veggie sandwich, found some granola bars for later, and even a bag of chocolate covered pretzels. She threw them in her bag and headed out the door in less time than she usually took to even decide on what to eat. She locked up thc house and walked toward the historic Old Town section of Rogue.

First stop, Sleepy Folk. It didn't open until later tonight, but the speakeasy had a pie shop as its front and it was open for lunch. Mmm. She could grab a couple of fried hand pies to take with her too. She'd leave a note there for Gal.

Heli knew she was headed into danger, and smart women always had a friend with a back up plan. Hopefully it would be too late for Gal to stop her, but she wanted someone to know where she'd gone in case she didn't come back.

The pie shop was hopping when she got there, so she skipped buying the fragrant pies. Besides, Kosta would smell them from a mile away and she wasn't wasting any of

Selena's no-smell perfume on dessert. Heli slipped up to the counter and shoved the envelope into the till. The cashier would find it and give it to Gal. Later, much, much later.

Kosta's strip club was a couple more blocks up the street, right at the edge of the district. It wasn't a creepy or slimy place like one would think a strip club would be. Kosta kept the riff-raff out and the place crystal clean. It was really more like a dance club that happened to have strippers for entertainment. He even had male review nights especially for the ladies. It was all very Magic Mike.

Heli crossed the street and grabbed a table at the little coffee shop. She could watch the front door to see when Kosta left.

Shoot. Except what if he went out the back which he probably would. Duh.

She walked all the way down the block again before she crossed just in case he happened to be looking out the front door for some unknown reason. Yeah, she was being paranoid. A few more doors down and she slipped between two buildings to the alleyway and then made her way back toward the Naughty Wolf.

The back alley was not nearly as nice as the shady outdoor seating at the coffee shop. She was seriously re-thinking the leather jacket and knee high boots. With the afternoon sun coming on, she was going to melt. It's not like she could order out for a cold drink. Plus, she didn't even see a place to hide so Kosta wouldn't spot her the second he walked out the door.

Oh god. Except that garbage dumpster over there. She was not getting into it. No way, except, she did have that spray. No, no, no. That wasn't a good use of the little she had. There were a few cardboard boxes in the recycling dumpster next to the bin. She'd simply build herself a little homeless person shelter.

After a lot of grunting and sweat and a few choice swear words she had enough broken down boxes so she didn't have to sit on the ground and could make a shield from the sun if she shoved them all between the two dumpsters. She stood in the doorway to the club and admired her work. It definitely looked like a pile of crap someone hadn't taken the time to throw away.

She slipped behind the recycling bin and into her stake out hut. She couldn't see great, but there were enough holes between the boxes that if someone as big as Kosta came out, she wouldn't miss him. Now to wait.

Twelve hours, two granola bars, a six pack of pamplemousse La Croix sparkling water from the convenience store, three really, really fast pee breaks, and five melted chocolate pretzels later and there was no sign of Kosta. The club was hopping though and she'd never known him to miss a Saturday night at the club. She was eighty-seven percent sure he was in there. Closing time was in two more hours, so she supposed she was stuck here until two in the morning. Just enough time for a nap.

Zara wouldn't nap if Heli was missing.

Maybe she should go buy an energy drink. Maybe she should go home.

Zara wouldn't go home.

Heli sighed and that turned into a yawn. She'd worried about four billion times in the past few hours whether this was really the right way to find her sister. She was this close to just going into the club and begging Kosta to help her. Maybe she could bribe him by promising to dance for him. She'd taken Helena's classes for a good month. Four lessons was plenty to do a good set of sexy moves on the pole.

"Hey, you smell something funny?"

"No. You're smelling your upper lip."

Two deep voices she didn't recognize came from just out of her sight to the left. She whipped out the bottle of no-smell and gave herself a quick squirt. If these guys were wolf shifters, she'd be pissed if she was discovered this late into the game. If they weren't, hopefully the perfume's effects lasted a while. She'd find out either way soon enough.

"Kosta's gonna be pissed we came back for him. I don't really feel like getting my ass kicked. Are you sure Decker is going to be impressed by this?"

"Totally. He was mad he was going to have to wait. So if we show up with this Troika in tow, he'll probably let us have our pick of the next group of women that comes through before he sells them."

Heli gasped and then covered her mouth. Shoot. Had she seriously just heard that? Another pack was buying and selling women? Were they involved in sex trafficking?

God. Zara could have been sold. Her stomach clenched. Heli was going to be sick.

She pressed her hands hard against her lips and swallowed six or seven times to hold back the bile rising up in her throat.

Kosta was going to flip his top. Being in an industry full of a lot of abuse, he'd worked hard since he opened the doors of the Naughty Wolf to make sure he had a safe place for his ladies to work. Zara had even told her that he donated money to the legal defense fund for the abused women she worked with. His mama raised him right.

Not like these two schmoes. Heli actually hoped they were wolves that were involved in Zara's kidnapping just so she could rip their balls off later. If they weren't? Well, then, after she found Zara and brought her back home, she'd find the assholes next and rip their balls off.

Grr. Being around wolves must be rubbing off on her, because she was feeling the need to go all teeth and claws on these guys.

The back door to the club opened and a blast of music and the sounds of people rolled out, along with Kosta. Heli snuck up closer to the holes in the cardboard to see him. Why did he always look so damn lickable? It was the beard and all the things he could do to her with it.

Geez. Much more thinking like that and she was going to have to use that whole bottle of perfume to mask her scent. Between her legs.

Kosta folded his arms and she swore he looked right at

her. "Did you seriously think I wouldn't know you were out here?"

Oh no. He wasn't talking to her, was he? She quickly, but carefully backed up so she couldn't see any of them anymore, only listen.

"We were counting on it, Troika."

"I don't like being spied on. This is not the way to win my help."

Heli's ribs tightened and her heart felt like it was shrinking right in her chest. He was talking to the crepoids, but the words were for her. He'd let her sit out here in the heat and garbage all day long full-well knowing she was here. Crap on a cracker. There went that plan. What was she going to do now?

KILLER WHALES AND OTHER SEA WOLVES

Yeah, he'd let Heli sweat out behind the club all day. At least he knew where she was the whole time and she wasn't getting into trouble. Guess she didn't know he had security cameras all around the Naughty Wolf. He'd watched her climb in and out of her little cardboard cave all day and chuckled every time. She thought she was so sneaky, it was cute.

Indulging her little game meant she was in trouble now. If the Bay pack enforcers even caught a whiff of her intoxicating arousal, she was either dead, or worse. How the hell she was turned on sitting amongst garbage having sweated her ass off all day was beyond him. Unless it was the element of danger that was getting her all hot and bothered.

If the two of them survived the night, he was going to remember that and use it against her in all the most fun ways. Until then he needed to distract the Bay pack enforcers so they didn't discover her. "Come inside, you can wait at the bar until I'm ready to go."

"We'd rather suck a bag of dicks," one of them said with a shit ton of nastiness dripping off each word.

Kosta growled at them and let his fangs descend. They might not have learned any respect in Bay, but they were on his turf. "That can be arranged."

The other one raised his hands and took a step back. "Don't make this hard, Troika. You've already made Decker wait long enough. Let's go."

He'd been prepared to offer them drinks on the house, but now it would sound like he was weak and bargaining with them. Dammit. He was going to have to fucking go with them. Much longer and they'd finally get the brown out of their noses and catch Heli's scent. "Fine. Get your ride, I'll follow you."

"How do you know we didn't run here in our wolf forms?"

Kosta grinned and pointed to the two corners of his building and then over the back door. "Security cameras. They're everywhere."

He looked right at Heli through the breaks in her cardboard box. He couldn't see her reaction, but enjoyed imagining her shock. Her face was probably similar to when she orgasmed. He loved that face.

Shit. No he didn't. He really, really liked that face. He had to keep love out of his relationship. He already had way too many flowery emotions for her. He had to lock that down and concentrate on keeping her safe and taking down the Bay asshats.

"You can ride with us then. Decker doesn't let any wolf approach the pack house in human form anyway, so you might as well leave your car here."

Good try, boys. "Fuck off. I'm not getting into your POS. Decker wants a wolf, that's what he'll get."

Kosta pulled his Naughty Wolf t-shirt over his head and tossed it onto the pile of boxes Heli was hiding behind. His clothes would help mask her scent. She already smelled like him, so if the dumbasses scented anything, they wouldn't think it was more than him they were scenting. The Bay enforcers followed suit and in another minute he was naked and letting his wolf come out to play.

While he waited for the other guys to finish their shift, he lifted his leg and peed on the boxes. Heli could kill him for his little golden shower later. Because she would be alive and that's what mattered.

The enforcers took off and right before he followed them, he spoke into Heli's mind. *Stay out of trouble until I get back,* ziaka.

She replied in her head with a whole litany of curses about his manhood. They made him chuckle. He was just happy she was alive and not in the clutches of Decker. If she'd been taken, this little war was going to turn into a huge ass personal vendetta on the Bay. They'd rue the day they touched his woman.

Shit. There he went again. He hadn't claimed Heli.

Mark her. Claim her. Mate her.

His wolf knew exactly what it wanted. His wolf needed to get fucking right in the head. Its animal instincts were off base this time. Not that they ever had been before. Kosta sprinted down the alley before he could think about the implications of that for even another second.

It was time to get in the game and that meant keeping Heli out of his mind. No more Heli. No. Heli.

Chastising himself like a dog should do the trick. Sort of. Not really. What he needed was some action to focus on. A good fight. Blood and guts. He might get that sooner rather than later. They ran along a patch of land that skirted the ocean and a large swath of forest. Nestled against the trees was his destination. They were approaching the Bay pack house, which was the old Bay Hotel.

What a shithole.

Kosta slowed down and surveyed the area. The building itself looked like an old-fashioned beach resort, the kind that were dotted all along the Eastern seaboard in the early 1900s. But the faded yellow paint sat chipped and falling off so it appeared more aged than sunny, and the shingles on the roof were in serious need of replacing. He was surprised the state park hadn't made them clean it up, or condemned it.

The enforcers didn't stop and wait for him. They went straight inside assuming he'd follow. Stupid.

He'd probably only have a minute or two to sniff around before they figured out he wasn't on their tails, but that would do. Kosta loped along the west side of the building and caught the scent of humans. Women. Dozens of lingering trails, most tainted with fear, rage, and disgust.

What the hell were these wolves doing with that many human women? Whatever it was, it wasn't good. One more reason to take them down.

One scent was fresh and the woman attached to it was nearby. Maybe he should try to rescue her now. Even if that would blow the rest of his plan, it might be worth it to get her out, and find out what she knew about their operations.

Kosta silently padded toward her, following her scent trail and soon the sound of her voice. Before he could make out the words, he could tell she was angry. He also caught a whiff of a man, a dirty one. Pure human, the kind that didn't take care of himself. But this woman wasn't afraid of him. She was pissed though.

He crept close, keeping to the trees and underbrush to stay hidden, until he could hear their conversation.

The woman was chastising the crap out of the guy. "Don't fuck around this time, Gerry. I got you off his shit list after you let the last batch get taken by that pack of do-gooders. He wanted to kill you, you know?"

Do-gooders. Interesting. Not all the packs on the East Coast had blamed the Troikas for starting the pack war. Maybe they had an ally he didn't know about.

Hat in hand, Gerry couldn't even look her in the eye. "I know, Vi. I won't screw up again. I promise."

"Good. Tell me the plan so I know you got it this time." It was very clear who the alpha was in this relationship.

"Bring the women to the front door, not the side door, like I'm supposed to." He recited his lines like a schoolboy wearing the dunce cap, trying his best to get out of the teacher's ire.

"What time?" she prodded.

"Exactly at midnight."

Maybe it was fortunate that the enforcers had come to get Kosta earlier than he'd planned. He would have missed this little conspirators' meeting. Now he'd be going into the Bay pack with more information than they wanted him to have.

"Not a minute past. You got it?"

Gerry took a couple steps backward to make his escape from the woman. "I got it, Violet. I'll be there."

"Make sure you are. Now get out of here before one of them smells you." Violet took out a pack of cigarettes and lit one. She puffed on it to get it burning hard and blew the smoke out after Gerry's retreating form. Tobacco smoke's overwhelming aroma interfered with a wolf's ability to smell anything else.

Kosta didn't doubt Vi knew that. She was smart and had questionable morals. He'd need to keep an eye out for her. He backed away, ready to go up to the front entrance. The enforcers would be out looking for him any second now.

Violet crushed her cigarette out on a tree and stuck the butt into her pocket. "I know you're there wolf. You can come out."

Well, shit. Kosta moved out from behind the tree, took

a few steps toward the woman and then sat, studying her to see what she would do.

She looked him over and gave a little jerk of her chin. "You a loner looking for a pack?"

Kosta tipped his head to the side, letting her make her own assumptions about his answer to her question.

"I can help you get into Bay. They're a powerful pack. Decker, the alpha, is going to be the most powerful wolf in America soon, maybe the world. You'd be smart to get on his side."

Decker? The new Wolf Tzar? Yeah, right. But it made sense for why his pack was making trouble and recruiting him. If a piece of shit like that ever became ruler of wolfkind, the world would go to hell in a fur-lined handbasket.

"But you have to help me too. I don't want anyone knowing about that conversation with Gerry. How about this?" She crossed her arms and raised her chin to look down on him. "You keep your mouth shut about that and I won't tell Decker you were out here spying on him."

Wow. Manipulation much? Kosta couldn't help but wonder how long this Violet had been with the Bay pack. Had she learned to be a bitch because of them or had they taken her in recognizing a skill they could exploit?

"I sure hope you're smarter than you look, wolfboy. If you're in, follow me and play along. If you're not, run, because I'll send the enforcers after your ass."

She must be close to Decker himself if she thought she could talk to a wolf-shifter that way. There was a third alternative in her ultimatum. If he were a true one-blood, she'd be dead. They didn't take kindly to getting orders from a human, especially a woman.

Violet sounded like she didn't care one way or the other what his response was, but her body language said different. Her shoulders weren't as relaxed as she thought they were and there were lines around her mouth that would become wrinkles as she got older. She was playing a long game here and it was taking a toll.

He would probably be doing her a favor if he growled and scared her away, in essence telling her to fuck off. Eventually some wolf would. He couldn't bring himself to beat her down. He stood and turned toward the house, waiting for her to take the lead. Letting her bring him in the house would be better than those two dumbass enforcers anyway.

Violet let out a pent up breath he wasn't supposed to notice, so he pretended he didn't. He trotted alongside her until they got to the door. It was set up so man or wolf could hit the handle to get in, which he had to admit was a good idea. The door swung open before either of them had a chance to push it.

"Where the fuck have you been?" A mountain of a man stood in the doorway glaring at Violet. Decker Kasatka, also known as the alpha of Bay pack.

Kosta held back the growl building in his throat. He wasn't here to kill Decker, because that would make him the alpha of Bay. Kosta was no alpha. No, he was going to destroy the pack from within so there was nothing left for Decker to be alpha of.

"Look, I brought you a present." Violet pointed at Kosta.

Decker glanced down at him and then waved them both in. He crossed the room and sat on a huge red overstuffed chair, like it was his throne. "Come to me, Troika. Shift to your human form and let everyone here see that one of the Troika brothers has come to join the Bay pack, the strongest pack in the world."

The men standing around in various states of undress, with women on their laps or sitting at their feet, howled for Decker's declaration.

Kosta rolled his eyes, but hid it in the midst of his shift. They wanted to see him. Here he was in all his glory. He let all of his wolf sink back into his body, except for his claws and fangs. A few of the ladies gasped and averted their eyes, but more openly stared. Violet licked her lips.

"I'm here, Decker. Whether I join you or not remains to be seen. I've got a lot going for me in my own pack, what more can you offer me?" All truths and questions. Nothing that should tip anyone off to his ulterior motives.

"Some fucking pants for starters." Decker gave Violet a shove and she scrambled to stay on her feet. She did though, and opened a tattered wicker chest against the wall. She tossed him a torn but clean pair of cut-off sweats. They'd be a bit tight on him and he suspected she chose them for that reason specifically.

He pulled them on and yeah, they weren't a whole lot better than being naked. The shape of his cock was clearly visible through the thinning grey material. Not that he was modest or anything. Wolf-shifters got over that pretty young, but he didn't like feeling used either.

"Violet." Decker snapped his fingers and pointed to his feet. Violet scurried back and dropped to her knees in front of him. He grabbed her jaw and angled her face to look up at him. "Who do you belong to?"

"You."

Belonged? Kosta didn't like the sound of that. He wasn't one to kink shame, but he doubted this was a Dom/sub thing. It would be different if she was his mate, but while she smelled like Decker, and had a bite mark on her neck, it hadn't formed into the tattoo of a mate's bite.

"That's right and don't you forget it." He pushed her aside and stared at Kosta. "Don't even think you can touch my fuck toys. There's plenty of pussy here for you and by the scent of all these whores in the room, you won't be hard pressed to get your dick wet. Stay away from Violet."

Christ. He had to make sure Decker didn't think he had any interest in that girl. Time to take this conversation in another direction. "I'm not much interested in humans. I'm surprised you are. I thought you lot were one-bloods."

Decker spat on the floor. "You must not have had your taste of a human woman's pussy, or had the rush of marking one. My bite turned Violet here into a psychic."

Kosta was familiar with the phenomenon. There were already a half-dozen or so humans in the Troika pack with wolf mates. Biting a human was punishable by death. Max had flouted that law because he'd found his one true mate. Decker had apparently done it for funsies.

Not all the human mates in the Troika pack had developed abilities. Some had become shifters themselves. Kosta had to consider that Decker didn't yet know that could be a side effect. Except Violet didn't have a real mark of a mate. Just the scar of a wolf's bite.

"Interesting that you would bite a human. Is she your mate?" He purposefully spat the word mate as if it disgusted him.

Decker stood up so fast his E-Z boy throne skidded across the floor. "We don't mate humans. You'd do well to remember that Troika."

"Why do you think I'm here?" The longer Kosta was around these guys the more and more he saw his mother and brother's point of view. Only fucktards thought like these one-bloods.

"That's a good question." Decker turned back to Violet, who was watching their conversation very closely. "You didn't predict for me whether he was coming or not."

Violet blinked too many times. "I, uh, you know my powers don't work that way. I can't control..." She got a dreamy kind of blank look in her eyes and then started shaking violently.

"Jesus. Is she having a seizure?" Kosta moved to help her, wracking his brain to remember any sort of first aid training. Something about protecting her head, don't stick anything in her mouth.

Decker stuck out his arm to block Kosta. "Don't touch her. She's having a vision."

If this was a vision, he was never biting a human. This wasn't a gift, it was a curse. Violet shook for another few moments and as her body released her, she groaned.

Decker approached and stood over her waiting for her body to still. When the last of the shakes stopped, he squatted down. "What did you see? What are the two paths?"

Violet took several deep breaths and pointed to Kosta. "He is either the bringer of good fortune to the pack, or a betrayer. You will know at the stroke of midnight."

Midnight, huh? One-hundred-and-one percent this was a fucking set up. Violet wasn't a psychic, but at least her game was about to work in his favor.

Decker looked at an old-fashioned cuckoo clock hanging askew on the wall. They only had about ten minutes to wait. "Boys, surround him. If that clock strikes twelve o' one and we don't have some kind of new fortune in our laps, kill him."

Shit. Gerry better not be fucking late.

Eight Bay pack enforcers from around the room stood up, leaving their women, and surrounded Kosta. One of them narrowed his eyes. "You don't look nervous, asshole. You should be."

He had to be careful what he said here. He couldn't outright say he wasn't going to betray the Bay pack because they would scent his lie. "I know what I am and what I'm not."

Tick, tick, tick. The room fell silent as every eye except Violet's watched the clock. Five minutes. Four. Three. Two. One. The clock made a buzzing sound and a sad and tired looking bird popped out of the door and sang his repeating song.

After ten cuckoos and no Gerry, Kosta got nervous. He made eyes at Violet and she gave him a Gallic shrug. The last two chirps of the bird went off and it retreated back into its house.

Fuck. Things were about to get ugly.

REVENGE IS BEST SERVED WET

A. Heli sure as shit hoped that perfume was working, because otherwise she smelled like wolf pee.

B. She was going to strangle Kosta when she caught up to him.

C. Did she mention the strangling?

She'd been smart enough to keep quiet when those other werewolf dudes had shown up. As soon as they were gone she'd screamed every curse word she could think of and invented a few new ones.

He'd let her sit in the hot sun behind a garbage can all day, and unless he was actually rescuing Zara from the pits of hell at this very moment, she was going to murder him in the face. As soon as she found him.

She marched home, changed her clothes, and got in Kosta's truck. She'd seen which direction they'd run, but would going south really do her that much good? Okay, think. Where would another pack of wolves live?

Wolves liked woods and stuff. The Troikas ran all over the Reserve. Gal said the Grimm pack used the arboretum for their outdoorsy wolf stuff. So another pack must have some kind of place like that. What woodsy area was south. There was the big state park down by the bay. It was a total long shot that she'd find him or Zara, but she had to try.

She started up Kosta's truck and hit the road south. There weren't a whole lot of other cars on the road this late at night, and there was no one in the golf club's parking lot. There were cars down by the marina, but this whole area didn't seem like the kind of place wolves would hang out unless they liked to swim and fish. Were sea wolves a real thing?

In another couple of minutes she went through the toll plaza and into the main park. She drove around and around the big roundabout three times trying to decide which way to go. The sign said the fields were to the left and the cottages and the old Bay Hotel were to the right. The hotel had been closed for longer than she was alive but no one had ever torn it down.

Hmm. That sounded like a good hideout for the underbelly of the werewolf world. She went to the right and when she saw the cottages, she parked Kosta's truck around the back of the closest one. If the bad guy wolves were here, she didn't need to announce her arrival with its loud engine. She grabbed her little backpack and hid the truck keys under a rock behind the front tire. She'd read about someone doing that in a book once and it had later saved their lives after their stuff had been taken away from them.

Heli flicked on the flashlight in her taser combo, then thought better of it. She didn't want anyone seeing the light and she might need the battery to tase the bad guys. Or Kosta, the rat.

The hotel was closer than she suspected. The side appeared just after she pushed through a group of trees. This was totally a bad guy hang out. There were lights on. Not a lot of them, and only on the ground floor, but there shouldn't even be electricity, much less people using it.

She stalked closer, glad that this time she'd chosen to wear sneakers instead of those badass, but not all that comfortable, boots. The thought that the occupants of the hotel could be teenagers out looking for a party place, or the for real mafia, only flitted through her mind.

A chorus of howls rang out from inside the building. "Aha," she whispered to herself. "I knew it, God, I'm good. I should start a detective agency."

Heli scurried through the small grouping of trees until she was so close, she could taste the cigarette smoke in the air. She crouched down so no one looking out a window would see her and wrinkled her nose. Gross. She smacked her tongue against her mouth. It was like a cigarette was right over her head.

"Gotcha." Someone grabbed Heli by her ponytail and yanked her up.

Her eyes watered from the pain of having her hair

wrenched like that. Her fight for her life reflex jump started and she elbowed the grabber. Except she didn't. Her elbow met nothing but air.

Her attacker laughed and kicked her feet out from under her and jerked her around by the hair again. He pushed her face into the dirt and grabbed her arm, locking her wrist into some kind of restraint.

Heli kicked and thrashed about, but didn't scream. She didn't want anyone else coming out to help her attacker. Someone nearby squeaked and Heli whipped her head around to see who was there.

Her stomach turned into crumbling black rock.

Tied to a tree was a line of women, dirty, bruised, and beaten down. The one nearest the front shook her head and mouthed the word "stop" to her.

Dear God. Was this what had happened to Zara? Was she looking into the eyes of her own future?

Her smelly attacker captured her other wrist and she wrenched herself away from him. If she could just get to her knees she could get some leverage, or sit on him. Her big butt had to come in useful sometime in her life. If not now, then never.

"Don't fight. It won't help," one of the women said in a dull, lifeless voice.

"Help me," Heli pleaded.

One by one the women turned their faces away from her.

Seriously? The attacker clamped the other side of his

restraint around her wrist and the clink of metal made Heli sick to her stomach. She tugged on her arms, but she couldn't budge.

"Hold still and this will be easier on you, lady." He stood and grabbed her by the shoulders but he wasn't strong enough to lift her up.

That gave her the leverage to get to her knees, but without her arms, she couldn't get her balance to stand. "I'm not holding still so you can rape me."

She got her first look at the guy. He was as dirty as the women and wore a shirt from a garage or gas station or something that had his name on a patch sewn to the front. "That's disgusting. Don't you know nothin'? You'll choose to be with them and you'll like it."

"Gerry." She'd heard if you called an attacker by name and gave them yours it would appeal to their humanity in some way. She needed to create a connection with him. "Gerry. I'm He–Hannah. You don't want to do this. I promise."

He glared at her. Maybe he'd bought that trainwreck of a shirt at a thrift store or something. "You ain't on drugs are ya? Decker don't like crack whores. You don't seem like one of them. In fact, he's gonna like this pretty blonde hair. He might even finally turn me for bringing him a nice piece of ass like you."

"Turn you?" Like turn him in? Did he want to get caught?

"You'll see. Come on." Gerry drug her up by her arm

and wrapped the dangling end of the rope from the last woman's wrists around her neck. "That's a slip knot that will just get tighter if you fight against it. So don't."

Gerry glanced down at his arm. "Shit, we're late. Fuck, fuck, fuck. Come on."

He gave Heli a shove and the rest of the women scooted forward. He grabbed the wrists of the first woman in line and ran up the steps. "I'm here. Hey, Decker. I'm here and I brought you a new batch. Even got a surprise."

Heli heard growls and snarls coming from inside and then a voice that shouted, "Hold. Get your ass in here, Gerry. Let me see what you brought. I'm thinking it might be our fortune."

"Oh, it is, your highness," Gerry said.

Your highness? This dilapidated hotel didn't seem like much of a castle for a king. Did wolves even have kings? Gerry dragged the string of women into the room and Heli was forced to clomp along after them or be choked. The light inside was a heck of a lot brighter than outside and she had to scrinch her eyes against the bare lightbulb hanging from the ceiling. She blinked a bunch of times and looked around.

They were in the gutted out lobby area of the hotel. These wolves were the worst decorators. They'd thrown together old couches and tattered chairs into a sort of living room setting. At the front, where the check-in desk probably used to be, was a really big man sitting in a red lounger kind of chair like it was a throne.

The king. She expected him to be some kind of hillbilly

poor white trash, but he was good-looking. Like some kind of backwoods underwear model just waiting to be discovered. That had to be how he'd convinced all these other guys standing around that he was their king.

While his looks were extraordinary, he was no Kosta. This guy had something mean in his eyes that gave Heli twitchy muscles, especially in her legs. They wanted her to run away from him. Far, far away.

Another glance around the room to see if there was an escape route besides the door they'd come in made the slip knot around her neck feel more like a noose. There were a lot of rough and tumble men, but there were also more women with that dead look in all their eyes.

That's when she spied Kosta. He was standing off to the side and breathing hard. He was flanked on either side by a half-dozen men, a couple who were bleeding from cuts on their faces or from their noses. Holy cow . They'd been fighting, and by the looks of it Kosta was winning. Had he been captured by them too?

He gave her a dark look and the tiniest, almost imperceptible shake of his head. Ugh. He didn't want her to acknowledge that they knew each other. Okay, she got it. They were both under cover.

"Well, well, well, Troika. Your luck just changed. Gerry did indeed bring us a fortune. Especially this new girl. Look at that ass. It's practically begging to be spanked."

Wait, was he talking about her? "Don't you even think about touching my ass."

The underwear king stood up and approached her.

"Ooh, a feisty one. My Violet used to be feisty too, didn't you, Vi? I do love taming a challenge. You will be fun."

He looked over his shoulder at a woman about Heli's age, or maybe a smidge older like Zara. The woman was glaring daggers of doom, dangerous and deadly death at Heli. Vi was not going to be an ally.

Decker chucked her under the chin and took a step back to address all the women. "You all have a week to prove yourself to the pack. If you're useful to me and my wolves, we'll keep you. If you're not, you'll be sold to another pack. But I'll warn you, no other pack you go to will be as powerful as mine."

Heli rolled her eyes. Can we say egomaniac?

Several women all tried to speak at the same time.

"I'm good with children. I have no problem with dirty diapers."

"I can clean and do your laundry."

Kosta used the distraction to grab her arm and pulled her close. He whispered low under his breath while looking around to make sure no one was taking notice of them. "What the fucking fuck are you doing here, Heli?"

Holy cow, he so mad he was growing tufts of fur out of the back of his neck and along his shoulders. Maybe he really had defected. Maybe he didn't care about her and didn't even want her here. Maybe all those feelings she thought they shared were a big pile of poo. She couldn't afford to worry about that. "Trying to save my sister."

"You could have been killed. I don't know how the fuck

I'm going to get you out of here, but until I do, don't let anyone even think that we know each other. Got it?"

Heli jerked her arm away and Kosta turned his back on her like he was super interested in looking out the window.

"I can garden," one girl offered quietly.

Underwear King glared at the gardener. "We don't have a garden. We aren't rabbits."

Gardener shrank. "Umm. I can, umm, type?"

Everyone in the room laughed, the men a lot louder than the women. They all laughed even louder when the King slapped gardener girl across the face. "You'll be assigned to the cleaning crew."

All eyes, except Kosta's turned toward Heli. She was the only one who hadn't volunteered a skill. "How about you, little chubby-wubby? Got any skills besides eating bon-bons and watching soap operas all day?"

Really? Bon-bons? Soap operas? What a douche. "I'll have you know I'm an excellent pastry chef, thank you very much."

One of the other men asked, "What does that mean?"

"It means she cooks good, dummy," someone else answered.

Underwear King looked her up and down. "Yes, of course. Never trust a skinny cook. Isn't that what they say? You must be a real good one."

She was officially changing his nickname in her mind from Underwear King to Douchepotato King. "Like I said, I'm a pastry chef. I can fulfill all your patisserie needs."

"If that means you can cook a rare steak with a side of steak with some steak on top, you can cook for us."

"I don't do meat. Except bacon because that is a gift from God no matter what religious people say. Especially glazed with maple and baked into chocolate chip cookies." She was not kowtowing to this misogynistic meat-eater.

"Cookies are not steak. Either you learn how to grill up some prime USDA Grade A beef or you get to be on the cleaning crew with Miss green thumb up her ass."

Gardener girl squeaked.

"Decker," a voice floated down from the grand staircase up to the second floor of the hotel. The sound reminded Heli of the Queen of England. All eyes in the room turned toward the darkened stairs. The only thing Heli saw was the yellow glow of wolf eyes. "I claim the *ponchik* as my helpmate. I could use someone who knows how to make me a nice *vatrushka* as I lay dying."

Douchepotato King rolled his head all the way back, like this woman had just asked him to give up his favorite toy. "*Da, mamochka*. You can have the chubby girl."

"*Spasiba, rybka.*" The eyes bobbed down the stairs until a white haired woman who looked more like Meryl Streep in that devil fashion movie than the babushka Heli expected appeared. "Come here, girl."

She waved Heli toward her. "*Rybka,* get your man to untie her."

Douchepotato King snapped his fingers and Gerry undid the knot around her neck and undid the cuffs. Heli felt like she could breath a lot better now and wasn't only because she was freed. She crossed the room, giving Kosta one quick glance, but he was looking anywhere but at her.

The older woman took Heli by the shoulders and looked into her eyes, then she squeezed her cheeks. "Yes, you'll do fine. Come with me."

Heli followed the woman up the first few stairs. They paused about three up and the woman turned and winked at Heli. Then she addressed the room. "I'll probably die tonight, but if I don't my lady's maid here will be down to make me coffee in the morning. Take up her time, when she should be attending to me, and face my wrath."

Whoa. Okay then.

They went up to the top of the stairs and the woman sat down, patting the step next to her. "Sit, *ponchik,* this old hotel has weird acoustics and we can hear everything from right here, but they can't hear or see us."

Douchepotato King was speaking. Of course he was. He probably loved the sound of his own voice. "She should have died months ago. But she's taking her damn sweet time about it. I hear your mother is too, Troika."

Selena was totally not dying. She was only like fifty, why would she? Surely Kosta would have mentioned if she was sick or something. Although, he had kept the whole wolf thing from her, so maybe not.

The woman put a hand on Heli's knee and patted it. "Shh. I'll explain later."

"I expect my mother will outlive us all," Kosta replied.

"You Troikas. Good thing you're here now then. We should have a welcome to the pack party for you since you did bring good fortune for us."

They heard some scuffling around and then Douchepotato King spoke again. "Here you go, you bastard. Your pick of any of our human women."

"Oh no," Heli whispered.

Her babushka in Burberry stood and motioned for Heli to follow her. "We don't need to hear what happens next. It's better if you don't, I think."

Part of Heli wanted to stay to see what Kosta would do. God. What if he did pick one of the women and had sex with her? This was probably why he was trying to break up. He wanted to come to this horrible pack and run amok like the rest of the douches. It certainly didn't seem like he was here on some rescue mission. Zara wasn't even among the women.

Tears pricked at Heli's eyes and she wiped them away with the back of her hand. She would allow two whole minutes to feel sorry for herself and then she had to prepare a plan to escape this place.

Babushka opened a set of double doors at the end of the hallway and the world went from the dark and dank broken down hotel to the opulence of the roaring twenties. The room was lit with several candelabras, the furniture was worn but well maintained, and the big bed at the far end of the suite was truly fit for a king. In this case, a queen.

"Welcome to my suite, child. I've been waiting for you to show up for quite some time. Now sit and relax, we have some plans to make."

KISSES AND KILLERS

He was going to kill her. First he was going to kiss her, and then he was going to kill her.

"Your choice of the lovely ladies, or the not so lovely ladies, if you catch my drift." Decker elbowed him in the ribs and laughed like the creepy asshole he was.

"What if I want one of the new girls?" Kosta was this close to blowing his cover. There was no way he could allow Heli to be in this hellhole longer than absolutely necessary. By his measure, necessary ended a good ten minutes ago, right around the time she walked through the door.

"Nope. Those girls are off limits, to everyone. Nobody touches them until I say so. I'm not risking all our plans on you, or any other member of the pack, wanting to get laid. Besides, I saw you eyeing the one with the boobs and the ass. You know her?"

Fucking hell. He couldn't lie. He'd barely gotten out of a

beat down a minute ago, if Decker even suspected Kosta was lying, he'd be back to getting his face punched in. "I might have fucked her before."

Sweet baby Jesus, don't let her have heard that. Or this. "I've fucked a lot of women in Rogue. That's what they're around for, right?"

"You got that right."

Har, har, har. Not.

Sure, he enjoyed sex as much as the next guy. More if it was with Heli. But where were the women in these men's lives who taught them how to behave, the difference between right and wrong, and what real love was? Piotr Troika, his father, was no slouch when it came to raising his boys right, but Kosta's mother was the one who'd started a revolution based on being able to choose who one loved and mated.

Now that he thought about it, Decker's mom was the only wolftress he'd seen around.

"I'd rather have a wolftress in my bed. Where are they?" He looked around the room like he was going to find them. His senses told him the only females here were the humans.

"I've married a few of them off to solidify some alliances, and the rest I keep in the cottages. The only wolftress I allow in the pack house is the alpha's mate, and as you can see, I have not chosen mine yet. My mother is the exception because she was the late alpha's mate, and she will follow him into death soon enough."

The pack matriarch dying when the alpha died was an

old legend. Kosta hadn't heard of any wolftress actually doing that in modern times, if at all. He was wondering if other packs of one-bloods had this strange mix of old but also wanting to change the old laws. They were picking and choosing what they wanted to believe in like cherries.

Very scary cherries. He needed to learn how to crush them soon and screwing around with kidnapped human women wasn't the way to do that. If Kosta had one skill from his childhood, it was knowing how to push his older brother's buttons. Who knew that would come in handy in real life?

Kosta crossed his arms and gave Decker his so-bored look. "To be honest, man, I'm not here to fuck around. You've seen my place, I've got plenty of ass at home. I'm here because the Troikas are farting around with fated mate bullshit instead of taking advantage of the fall of the Volkovs. I thought your pack might be different, maybe I was wrong."

"You wanna get to work? That can be arranged. Because Bay pack is the future, Troika." Decker snapped his fingers and waved the women away. "Go do something productive. Get us something to eat. Troika here wants to see what we do and we're going to work up an appetite."

Once the women were gone, Decker went to a desk and unlocked the top drawer. He laid a map out and waved Kosta over. "Before I show this to you, I need to know if you're in. I'm looking for a second in command, someone I can rely on who isn't dumber than a box of rocks. You're that guy, Troika. You believe in the same things I do and together we can bring wolfkind out of the shadows. Are you with me?"

"Show me these plans to take over the world." It wasn't a yes, but Decker grinned at him like it was.

The map laid out all the pack territories from the coast to the Mississippi river and from the northern tip of Quebec to the Florida keys. It was the most comprehensive guide to packs and their domains he'd ever seen. Kosta doubted even the Volkov's had this much detailed knowledge.

"Where did you get this?" Kosta didn't have to force the awe in his voice. Local packs knew their own territories down to the last leaf, and usually knew the gist of where other packs that abutted them roamed, but that was about it. Pack politics was ever changing and so were their borders.

Decker leaned on the table, covering a portion of the map with his hands and looked right into Kosta's eyes. "You're not going to like the answer."

Probably not. "In for a penny, in for a pound."

Decker glanced around as if he didn't want everyone in the room hearing him and dropped his voice. "We killed a Crescent pack spy who was carrying it."

Crescent was a powerful pack. Selena had been trying to set one of the Troika boys up with Taryn Crescent, the daughter of their alpha since they were little kids. They were also the pack that had murdered his father and tried to take over the Troikas territory. "Ramsey must have a huge network to get this kind of intel. You think this is the basis of his plans to take over the other packs, or at least ally with them?"

"No. Here's the part that's gonna blow your mind. The spy swore Ramsey Crescent acquired the map when he killed your father. This is his map." Decker pointed dead on to the Troika pack territory. It was the only space not marked with the name of the pack or its alpha. "Looks like your dear old dad was keeping you out of the loop while he and your brother planned to take over the throne."

A cold chill seeped into Kosta and sank all the way to his core.

"Now you can see why so many other packs have marked the Troikas down as enemies. Planning a coup like this takes years. Your father wanted to be Tzar. Now his plans have fallen right into my lap and I'll get to lead wolfkind into a new era."

What in the actual fuck was going on?

Decker went through the map and which packs he'd already allied with, which packs were on the fence, and which were only going to join by force. He was practically salivating at the part of his plans where they made humans their slaves. He droned on and on about his world domination plan until the early morning light peeked in through the windows of the hotel's shutters. Kosta listened with half his brain. Another forty-five percent was going back and forth on whether he should take off the second he had a chance and bring this to Max or not.

Max was the new alpha of the Troikas. He probably already knew and was trying to implement this plan himself. Without Kosta. That didn't seem right. Maxim had never wanted to be alpha. He wouldn't want to be Tzar.

Had the Troikas' plans to rule died with his father? The thing was, his father was a Volkov loyalist. He towed the party line, followed the rules. Their mother on the other hand...

He needed more time to figure out what was really going on here before he talked to Max about all of this. Until then, his family needed to think he'd left them to join Bay.

The last five percent of Kosta's brain was fixated on Heli. It was the loudest damn part of his brain, too. He couldn't stop worrying about where she'd gone or what she was doing, and if she was hurt or in danger.

The distraction of her was going to get him into trouble and now, more than ever, the stakes were astronomical. He had to find a way to get her out of here and to safety. If he didn't, and he failed to take out Decker and the Bay pack, she and these women wouldn't be the only humans in danger.

Decker punched Kosta in the shoulder. "Are you even listening?"

"Yes. You want to get the rest of the packs on the island on your side and move into Jersey next to gather strength before moving north and taking on Crescent."

"Huh. I was sure you'd zoned out there." Decker narrowed his eyes. "What do you think about that plan?"

"I think we're gonna need more than Jersey to take on Crescent. They're the biggest pack on the Eastern

Seaboard and Ramsey is well respected. Any packs north of the Sound are probably already allied with him. You're not thinking big enough. If you want to be the wolf Tzar you need everything from here," he pointed to New Jersey and dragged his finger down the map all the way to South Carolina, "to here."

Decker whistled. "Then we've got a lot of work to do. We'll start tonight."

He pulled the map away and rolled it up.

Damn. There went any chance of absconding with it. "I'd like to study that some more."

"Nobody gets access to the map unless I'm around. We'll go over it again tonight. I'm beat and you look like you've been hit by a truck. Take any of the rooms on the third floor you want." Decker shoved the map back into the desk and turned the key to lock the drawer. "Violet. Let's go."

Violet had brought them food and drinks a couple of hours ago and then had laid down on a nearby couch, waiting for Decker. She stood and stretched and then walked over to the two of them. Decker grabbed her by the hair and kissed her hard. She groaned and wrapped her arms around his neck.

Ugh. Kosta had never been bothered by other people's PDA, but these two were disgusting. He backed away, not that he thought they'd notice. "I'm gonna go up."

He took the stairs two at a time and ducked into a dark alcove on the second floor. If he was supposed to be on the third, hopefully nobody would think to look for him here. His phone had been buzzing in his pocket for half the night. Decker wasn't half as dumb as he'd thought he was, but he hadn't been smart enough to take his only line of communication to the outside world from him.

Seven messages from Maxsim. Two from his mother. He hit the button to look at the ones from his mom first.

Pick up milk on your way home.

and

Coffee. I'm coming for coffee.

That was weird. His mother didn't drink milk and he'd seen her make coffee from a full bag yesterday morning when he'd taken Heli to their home. Also...Kosta didn't live at her house anymore, so she wouldn't have asked him to pick something up for her on the way home, regardless of what it was.

Weird. Maybe one of Max's four billion texts would explain.

Where the fuck are you?

What the fuck do you think you're doing?

Get the fuck back here.

This was going great so far. The one good thing about text messages was that Max couldn't use his alpha voice and compel Kosta to come back. That meant no answering the phone or even listening to voicemails from here on out.

He scrolled through the rest of the messages which all had pretty much the same gist but with more and more creative placements of the word fuck. It was the very last message that hit him in the gut. He'd known something like it was coming, but it still landed like a boulder in his stomach.

You're betraying everything we've ever known. Even Niko did what he did for good. You're being a selfish bastard. I won't forget this, little brother. You're dead to me.

Fuck indeed.

Well, good news. If anyone else happened to catch a glimpse of his phone it would play right into the story he was trying to sell that he'd left the Troikas. He stared at that message from Max for another full minute before he flicked the screen on his phone off. It took him several long minutes to catch his breath.

"Psst. Kosta."

He glanced up from the black screen and into the dark hallway. Heli's head was poking out a door near the end of the hall. She waved him toward her in that hurry up way.

He shook his head. There was already a chance some other enforcer coming up or down the stairs could catch him here. Alone, he could feign ignorance about not knowing where he was supposed to be going. But if they caught him with Heli, that would draw attention to the both of them.

"Everyone is going to bed, you need to get the hell out of here while you can." The rest of the women had been corralled and taken to the cottages hours ago. Heli had a prime opportunity. "I'll give you my phone and you can call Max to come get you."

"I have my own phone and I'm not leaving. Now come here." She waved him over more frantically this time.

Kosta looked around and listened for movement in their direction but didn't detect anyone. He shouldn't risk it, but he was going to because after the night from hell, he really wanted to hold her in his arms and know that she was okay. He didn't want to need her. But he did, he needed her like a wolf needs the moon.

It took less than five long strides to get to her and she opened the door, waving him in. She started to stay something, but he didn't give her a chance. He pushed her up against the wall and took her mouth in a long, hot, sensual kiss. Heli gave every bit of passion right back to him. She wrapped one leg around the back of his calf and pushed her hands into his hair.

Then she bit his lip. Hard.

"Ouch. What did you do that for?" He licked his lip but didn't taste any blood.

"That was for peeing on me."

He chuckled. "*Zaika,* that probably saved your life. You smell too sweet and delicious. They would have found you hiding in your boxes."

Heli stomped on his foot. "That's for letting me sit in the hot sun behind the garbage can all day."

Kosta picked her up and carried her over to the bed. "This is for following me out here and putting yourself in danger."

He dropped her and made sure she landed on her stomach with her soft ass in the air. She squeaked and tried to get away, but he held her down and gave her a good thwack on the butt. "Keep quiet or you'll bring the enforcers down on us."

"I'm gonna enforcer your face." She wriggled to get out

of his grip but all that did was make her ass look even more enticing.

He gave her another half-hearted tap on the ass. "Are you ready to go home, or do you need some more spankings?"

Heli rolled away from him and he let her go. If they were anywhere else, in any other situation, spanking her would be foreplay. Here it was too much of a reminder of how these wolves treated women. He wanted nothing more than to sink into her wet heat and have her whisper sweet nothings to him. Instead, he was going to do the right thing and find a way to get her home.

Heli scooted away and up against the headboard and held out a finger. "I can't go. Mariya, the queen mother lady, thinks she might know where Zara is."

"You can't trust her. This whole pack is dangerous. We have to get you out of here. Come on, let's see if we can sneak you out now." He'd have to avoid any questions about Heli being missing or risk blowing the whole operation. It was a chance he had to take. For her. He stood, but Heli grabbed his hand and held him back.

"No. Wait." Her big brown eyes stared up at him pleading and he couldn't resist her. "She knows your mom and she said you have to tell Selena, tea, not coffee, and that she has the milk. She said your mom would understand."

Holy shit. That changed everything.

CLUES TO SERENITY

Kosta was out on another one of Decker's secret missions and Heli was starting to get worried. He hadn't come back this morning and several other wolves had, all torn up.

He'd come back from the first trip out to visit the nearby packs with a cut on his leg that had taken a full day to heal. When they were in their wolf forms, injuries got better almost right away, so for this one to take so long kind of freaked her out.

He'd snuck into her little room that adjoined Mariya's during the day when the rest of the pack slept. He'd shifted into a wolf and curled up on a rug in front of the old school fireplace instead of crawling into bed with her like he had the first day they were here. She'd dragged the pillows and blankets down to the floor and snuggled up beside him.

He was gone by dusk when she woke up. Morning after

morning he came to her, but didn't touch her. He was exhausted from whatever it was he was out doing with Decker and the pack. The first few days he continued to try to talk her into escaping. Not the last two. He hinted that he had other plans now and she should just stay out of trouble.

Trouble was coming though. Tomorrow was the one week deadline Decker had given the women to prove themselves. Tomorrow Decker and the rest of the pack would be allowed to claim the women they wanted. If Kosta wasn't here, or worse, if he was dead, she didn't know what she would do.

Now, she sat in Mariya's room melting some chocolate over a little hot plate, biting her lip and imagining all the worst things that could happen to Kosta out there in the danger zone.

"*Ponchik,* chocolate is in short supply around here. If you burn that, I'll feed you to the wolves." Mariya gently chided her.

"Sorry. I–"

"I know. I've seen that look on many a young woman's face. I'm just glad yours isn't directed at my boy. He doesn't deserve someone as sweet as you." Mariya set the tray of madeleines waiting to be dipped in the chocolate on the small table.

Yikes. That had to be hard for a mother to say.

"You need to be careful around him. He has an eye for you, and I'm afraid your Kosta wouldn't take kindly to Decker marking you."

"I thought marking was something mates did." Gal had been marked by Max and now she had this badass looking moon tattoo on her neck. "Didn't he already mark Violet?"

"That's the way it works in polite society. The Bays haven't been polite for a long time now. Decker, and his father before him, bite any woman they want to claim for themselves. Even wolves that have fallen as low as the Bay pack won't touch a woman marked by another."

Oh no. Mariya had basically just admitted that her husband had also been a philandering asshole. No wonder she secluded herself away from the rest of the pack. It had been lucky for Heli too. She hadn't been made to interact with any of the wolves, except Decker whenever he came to check on his mother.

To check if she was dead yet, more like. Mariya did a good show of moaning and groaning like she was in pain whenever he came around. Heli hoped to someday repay the woman for helping to keep her safe.

"The wolves who brought us the flour and butter you asked for also brought me news. I believe it's about your sister."

Mariya wasn't a simple old babushka. Some of the wolves in the pack didn't like the way Decker ran things. They were loyal to Mariya because, while her mate had been a dick, he hadn't been much of an alpha. Not the kind that went around trying to take over the world. Thanks to Mariya, the Bays had their own network of friends, aka spies. Including Selena.

It seemed the wolftresses had their own secret codes for

communicating. That's what the weird messages about coffee and tea had been about. Females were allowed to have social gatherings, like tea and scones with each other, even during a pack war. Misogyny at its finest had been the basis of wolftress subterfuge from the beginning.

Food codes. Heli could definitely get down with that. She'd also had to promise Mariya she would never, ever, ever, reveal the code to any man, wolf shifter or not. Seemed the code had existed for generations purely because no wolftress had let her mate know about it.

Girl code. Fries before guys, tacos before pacos, basically foods before dudes. Cool.

"They brought me a note from Taryn Crescent." Mariya handed over an envelope made of fancy woven paper with a printed invitation to a high tea inside. "There's a note on the back."

Dearest Mariya,

I do hope you can come for tea. We've got the milk you wanted. It will bring such Serenity. Your companion may attend if you like. I can foresee we'll be like sisters. If you can't come, I'll send the milk along after the new moon. Father will want it back, mind you. He may even come for it himself.

That was the weirdest note she'd ever read. "I don't understand what this means."

Mariya pointed to the words. "This here means they have a human woman. I think she's saying the human is a prophet or seer, kind of like Violet. She also says the Crescents will launch an attack on Bay after the new moon."

"Uh, you got all of that from this?" Mariya had

explained before that coffee meant a friendly visit and tea meant the opposite. Milk meant human women. Heli scanned the note again trying to read between the lines.

Serenity.

Zara's full name was Zarenity.

Sisters.

It was too bizarre of a coincidence that Taryn used those words to not believe it was a message meant for Heli. It was too crazy to believe. How could her sister have some supernatural psychic abilities without Heli knowing? There was only one way. She'd been marked by a wolf.

Heli didn't know what to think and wished there was a way she could see this woman for herself. Kosta wanted her to escape. If she did, she was going straight to Cape Cod where this Crescent pack lived. He wouldn't like that part of her plan at all.

A knock sounded on Mariya's door. She rolled her eyes and crawled into her bed to fake dying some more. Heli waited until she was buried deep in the covers and then opened the door a crack. Instead of Decker she found Violet.

"We need your help in the kitchen." Violet tried to see around Heli into the room. "The men brought home fresh fish and game and want us to make a feast to celebrate their victory today. Everyone needs to help. Even you, princess."

Both Kosta and Mariya had warned Heli not to leave this room if she could help it. "I can't leave Mariya."

"She can pretend to die without you for a while." Violet

shoved the door open and grabbed Heli by the arm. She yanked her out into the hall and toward the stairs. "It's time you pulled your weight around here. Since you have such a fat ass, you should be doing more than the rest of us."

"Maybe if you had a little more junk in your trunk you wouldn't have to...umm... Crap. I can't think of a good insult, but I'll shout it out later when I do."

Violet didn't even respond to that. Heli was going to have to up her game around this one. Out in the real world they wouldn't be friends, but here in wolflandia, it would be smart for them to at least have each other's backs. That didn't seem likely so far.

When they got to the kitchen, Heli almost gagged. Laying on the table, the one she'd just scrubbed earlier today when she'd made the madeleines, was a huge hairy-ass pig thing and a pile of slimy fish. The boar or whatever it was had tusks and flies and smelled like poo. "I don't know what you expect me to do with that monstrosity. I said I can do things with bacon, not the lord of the flies."

Violet scowled at her. "You said you were a pastry chef and that means you went to culinary school."

"Yeah, to make really good cookies, cakes, pies, and chocolate showpieces. I'm mostly vegetarian for goodness sake." Gross. She was seriously going to throw up. It was a good thing no one had turned her into a werewolf like Gal. Who ever heard of a predator snacking on veggies and ranch dip?

"Figure something out. Decker specifically said you should cook it." Violet shook her head and shrugged. She was enjoying knowing Heli hated this. She'd probably put the idea into Decker's head in the first place.

Heli covered her mouth and nose and took several steps back toward the doorway, ready to flee. She ran into a wall of muscle. Muscle that belonged to Decker. A weirdly wet and sea salt smelling Decker. Had he caught those fish himself?

He grabbed her by the shoulder and led her back into the kitchen. "Yes. I did say that. You are a great help to my mother, and I appreciate that, but how will you contribute to the pack when she's gone?"

He chucked her under the chin like they were much more intimate of friends than they were. Heli jerked away, but that put her right into Violet's line of sight. If looks could kill...

"Umm. It's got to be butchered and while I know how to cook, I do not know how to butcher an animal or gut a fish. Sorry." She shrugged and tried to back away again. Of any two people in the world, she didn't want to be in a room with either of them. She'd rather be stuck with just the piggy.

Decker grabbed her by the arm and licked his lips, which was about as disgusting as the dead animal doing the same. How could she have ever thought this guy was good looking? The longer she knew him, the uglier he got.

"Listen close, woman. We are inviting a delegation of pack alphas from five states and we will have a feast for them. You will figure out how to prepare this animal and those sturgeon or I'll make you sorry."

Heli swallowed. The look in Decker's eyes was two things, lust and violence. The little hairs on the back of her neck stood up and that made her very uncomfortable. She needed to get his focus off of her and the best way to do that was to make him believe she'd make that damn pig into a meal. "When are they coming?"

Kosta came in and leaned against the doorway. Heli almost cried she was so relieved to see him. He was covered in blood, but he didn't appear to be injured. She looked at the dead pig and then at him. Oh, geez. He'd hunted this thing and brought it to her. She'd thank him for that later.

"Tomorrow night," Kosta said. "I'm not dumb, lady. We knew you'd need prep time."

Kosta glared at her like she was the worst kind of dumb. The level of disdain in his voice was a bit much. No way anyone was going to assume he liked her even a little bit. She got the message and played along. She stuck her tongue out at him.

Decker gave Kosta the guy head jerk of approval "Yes. So as my Violet said, figure it out. It's going to be one hell of a party and you're going to make it extra special, aren't you?"

Ooh. She did not like where this was going. Maybe if she had a month to research recipes, a working gourmet kitchen, and an experienced sous chef, she could figure out how the hell to make giant smelly dead animal delicious. They were carnivores that preferred their steaks raw, so maybe she just needed to get a big barbecue grill and throw it on there.

Something in the way Decker was still staring at her gave her the feeling he wasn't just talking about the food for this party. "I am?"

He smiled, which bared his teeth and she literally watched some pointy ass fangs descend. "Yes. You'll make a feast fit for a king and then I'll mark and claim you in front of all the alphas so they can see exactly the kinds of delights they can expect under my reign."

Violet's jaw dropped open. "Her? You cheating bastard."

Decker turned on Violet and smacked her across the face hard enough that she stumbled back. "You forget your place, woman. I am the wolf and you are a human woman. If I want to mark and fuck every women who comes through those doors, that is my right as an alpha."

Violet fisted her hands by her side and didn't reply. Heli's heartbeat suddenly developed a murmur, skipping beats. She wanted to go to Violet, but no one in the room moved.

"Kosta, get your former fuck buddy what she needs. You've done well for me so far, and I want this meeting to go off without a hitch. This could be the turn in the tide we need to catch the big fish." Decker stomped off.

"Whatever you need, Deck." Kosta remained at his position leaning against the door jam like he didn't give a crap. "Get out of here, Vi. You'll go make it up to him if you know what's good for you."

"Fuck off, Troika." Violet flipped him off, but hurried after Decker.

Neither she nor Kosta moved from their spots until they were both sure Decker and Violet were long gone. They heard a door slam somewhere nearby and Kosta was on her before the sound echoed through the room.

She wanted to tell him not to kiss her when he was covered in blood and there was a stinking dead thing that he'd killed nearby, but she couldn't. That conversation with Decker and the way he'd hit Violet scared the cheez-whiz out of her. She needed Kosta's strong safe arms around her until her heart quit skipping beats and raced for him instead of for her life.

He pulled away much sooner than she would have liked. But they both knew it wasn't safe to be caught together like this. "Babe, we have to get you out of here. No more stalling waiting on news of your sister."

"Wait. Mariya got exactly that, right before Violet dragged me down here. The Crescent pack has Zara and, they're going to attack Bay after the new moon. When is that? It doesn't happen to be before tomorrow night does it?" This could save her from Decker's creepy plans.

He stroked her hair and shook his head. "After."

He didn't seem that bothered by the news that another pack was coming to fight them. "Crud muffins. Guess I'm making a barbecue pig."

"No, we're getting you out of here." His eyes swirled with that purple glow. "I will not allow Decker to make a move on you, much less mark and claim you."

Mariya had told her that wolves wouldn't touch a woman marked by another wolf. "Then you mark me. You claim me. Decker won't touch me then."

"He'll also probably kill me." He laughed humorlessly. "No. We need to get you back to Troika territory."

She was so close to finding Zara. She couldn't leave now. "But the Crescents are coming. They have Zara."

That light in Kosta's eyes deepened, but his fangs didn't drop and no claws appeared. He was calm. "The Crescent pack isn't going to find anything when they get here, *ziaka*. The wolves that are coming tomorrow night are going to tear Bay apart."

"Whoa, what?" Geez. All this time, she'd wondered how he could be working for Decker and his nefarious plans, and he'd been creating this master plan to destroy the bad guy. He'd make a way better alpha than Decker ever would. Thinking of him being in charge of a pack, making them better warmed her inside in an unexpected way.

When Gal had killed the Grimm pack alpha that made her their new leader. Was Kosta going to become the alpha of Bay? Why did the thought of that make her so hawt for him?

"That's what I've been working so hard to make happen. Every pack we've gone to visit, Decker thinks he's convinced them he's going to be the new Tzar. A few of them with one-bloods as alphas are on board. But most aren't. I convinced those ones that together we can take Decker down. That's why they're all coming here and I don't want you around for that."

"I'm not going anywhere." She snuggled up closer to him. "If you're taking over this pack, I am so here for that."

"No, babe. I'm not an–"

She pressed a finger to his lips. No negative affirmations from him.

"I think we should invite your mom for tea."

THE BEST LAID PLANS

No matter how Kosta cajoled or pressured Heli, she wasn't going to budge. She wanted to be here for what she called his moment of victory. She was going to be disappointed when there wasn't some kind of declaration that he'd defeated Decker. The way she'd reacted to that stupid feral pig they'd captured on the way home from the Chincoteague pack meeting, he knew she wasn't down for the blood and guts that would come from a pack fight.

Throats would be ripped out, faces eaten off, bodies torn to shreds.

He was out of time to get her to safety. If he was lucky he'd get Mariya to lock Heli in her room. Kosta didn't feel real lucky.

Heli was out on the beach right now bossing a bunch of men around who had dug her a roasting pit and constructed a giant spit out of old plumbing parts. The way those guys did every little thing she said, and were happy to, made him both jealous and a little bit more in love with her.

Dammit. Yes. He was fucking in love with her. How could he not be? She was brave in the face of all she'd been through, smart as a whip, and his soul ached for her. Literally ached.

He couldn't believe Decker or any of the other enforcers hadn't smelled the need on him. He did his best to pretend to have heaps of disdain for her whenever she was around. They'd both been careful to not be seen together, and she'd done great limiting her exposure to the pack, but she'd been around for meal times and such and he'd seen the way Decker looked at her.

The pure greed made Kosta want to kick Decker's teeth in.

Whether she wanted to or not, Heli was leaving tonight. He'd already made arrangements with one of the incoming alphas to take her and get her to Max.

"Kosta." Decker signaled to him from the steps of the hotel. "The scouts have spotted the first pack incoming. It's show time."

Yes, it was. He jogged up to the hotel with his game face on. Within the hour, four packs' delegations had arrived. All except the Fire Island pack. The ones who were supposed to get Heli out.

Shit. No need to get worried yet, he kept telling himself. The knot in his gut said otherwise.

They had been a hard sell in the first place. Fire Island

were long time rivals of the Bay. It had taken Kosta three tries just to get close enough to their alpha to discuss the plan with him in the first place. They'd been the first pack he'd gone to and the last to agree. His leg was still tender from their response to him showing up. They didn't like other wolves in their territory.

So far, everyone played their part perfectly as they ate and drank together. Heli's roast boar stuffed with sturgeon and their caviar was a huge hit. The alphas discussed plans for the future with Decker, and no one gave even a hint they were there to destroy Bay. The plan was precise and until Fire Island showed up, no one was making a move.

The Chincoteague alpha, known as Teagan, signaled Kosta over. "Is this happening or not? I'm growing weary of Decker's arrogance."

Kosta could relate. "We may need to proceed without Fire Island. I've got men inside the pack loyal to me that can do their part of the plan."

"Then let's do this, Troika."

He didn't like being pushed into a half-assed scenario, but if it meant Bay would go down and Heli would be safe, he didn't see any other choice. "Spread the word. We go on my signal."

Decker stood up on his favorite chair in front of the gathered crowd. "Heads up, wolves. I've got a little surprise for you all. Gather round."

This better not be the part of the night where Decker tried to claim Heli. Shit. It probably was. He'd waited too long. He glanced around the room and didn't see her anywhere. Fuck, fuck, fuck. What had the bastard done with her?

Decker motioned to one of his enforcers who brought him a dirty cardboard box. Blood had leaked from whatever was in there, soaking one corner and the whole thing reeked. Decker opened the lid and peeked inside, then waved his hand in front of his nose acknowledging the stench for the room to see. Some laughed and others that were standing closer groaned.

Decker grinned. "I'd like to demonstrate for you all gathered here tonight, what kind of Tzar I will be. For those who are loyal to me, you'll have women and riches galore."

He waved his hand and Violet led a band of women, made up to look like happy hookers, into the room. Heli wasn't with them.

A smattering of mostly Bay wolves clapped and whistled. "Tonight, you'll have your pick of these little treasures and know that there are more where they came from. But while I will be a benevolent ruler, you should be aware of what happens to someone who betrays me."

Kosta didn't think Decker even knew what the word benevolent meant. Decker hadn't discussed any of this with him which was surprising as he'd worked hard to ingratiate himself and become the right hand man around here. He didn't like where this little dog and pony show was going, especially since he didn't know where Heli was.

The room fell silent and Decker continued. "I've suspected for a while that Bay pack had a spy amongst us.

Someone who was passing information to my enemies. I will not stand for that but I waited patiently to sniff him out."

He reached into the box and lifted out the decapitated head of Gerry. Poor schmoe. "I will act swiftly to ensure those enemies are destroyed."

Thank the moon goddess herself it wasn't Heli. Kosta half suspected Decker would kill his own mother if he found out she wasn't upstairs dying like she was supposed to be.

Decker paused a moment and looked at each of the alphas in turn, finally ending his stare down by looking directly at Kosta. He reached into the box and lifted out a second head. The room gasped and grumbled when he revealed the face of the Fire Island alpha.

"Sorry, Troika."

Oh shit.

"I know you thought we could count them as allies but they've been plotting against me for a long time and using Gerry here to gather information." Decker lifted the head into the air. "Fire Island is now a part of the Bay pack and will be forever more."

Several of the alphas in the room glared at Kosta, but Decker was having so much fun bouncing around on his throne of surprises that he didn't even take notice.

God, that was a close fucking call. Even without Fire Island, they could still take Decker down. Kosta didn't want to give the go ahead until he knew Heli was safe. He was going to have to slip away and try to find her.

"One more surprise for all of you. You've no doubt heard that Crescent has their own psychic. The Bay pack has one of our own. Violet come up here."

She looked nice and smug. That woman was trouble with a capital T. If something had happened to Heli, she was behind it. Kosta was going to kill her and eat her heart out with a spoon.

Decker smiled at them all. "Violet is the reason I knew about Gerry, and she's predicted several other scenarios that benefited our pack by knowing in advance. Swear your fealty to me, alphas, and I'll provide you with a human woman to mark like I have Violet. My sources say only true alphas' bites create these powerful psychics."

Teagan whispered in a low voice. "You didn't mention any of this to us, Troika."

Damn it. "Because it's all bullshit. Violet isn't a real seer, she's made it all up. I've been caught in the web of one of her fake visions before. Don't trust anything she says."

"Maybe it's you we shouldn't be trusting." Teagan growled.

Fucking great. They could take Bay down without Fire Island, but without Teagan's men, they were screwed. Everything he'd been working for was about to go tits up.

"I've been itching to try my hand at it again. Shall we see what happens when an alpha marks a human female?" There were more yeses from the audience than Kosta liked.

He was losing them. Suddenly none of that mattered because Decker motioned to the back and one of the enforcers brought Heli, wearing a dirty white mess that looked like an old wedding dress, through the crowd. "Let go of me, you asshat. That's the last time I give you any of my roast pig. I hope you choke on that illegal caviar. Or that it gives you high blood pressure at least."

Heli's words trailed off as she took in the sea of men and the line of women all watching her. She tugged at the too-tight bodice of the white monstrosity they'd put her in. Kosta moved to grab her from the enforcer's grip, but Teagan stuck out his arm to hold him back.

"I want to see what happens, Troika."

Kosta shoved Teagan's arm off and growled at him. He pushed through the crowd right to the front. If Decker fucking touched Heli, plans be damned, Kosta would kill him here and now and take over the Bay and Fire Island packs. Didn't matter if he wasn't a true alpha, he would become one for Heli.

Violet wasn't looking so smug anymore. She'd had her millisecond in the spotlight and was getting pushed aside now. She took one look at Decker's lust-filled face for Heli and went into full-on convulsions.

Lord love a drama queen. Kosta was going to use this in his favor. "Look, Violet is having another vision. We'd better wait and find out what she's seen."

Her convulsions didn't last nearly as long as last time. She opened her eyes, but they were milky white. Cool trick. "The woman before you is a catalyst. If she is claimed by one unworthy, the false mate will cause the destruction of his manhood and this pack. The one who claims her as his true mate will find only greatness. All will be revealed under the new moon."

Violet gasped and the strange sheen from her eyes faded. She coughed and grabbed her throat like she couldn't breath. No one moved to help her. They all just stared at Heli. She looked around at them wide-eyed and gave a little wave.

Teagan stepped forward, examined Heli, then looked between Kosta and Decker. "We will wait for the new moon to declare our fealty. No one makes a move until then."

Kosta grabbed Heli's arm and dragged her away from Decker. He had one shot to sell this. "No one's manhood is safe with her around. I'm locking this one in her room until then. We can't take the chance that some damn fool tries to claim her."

"Yeah. Good thinking. Guard her for me." For the first time since coming to Bay, Decker looked a bit shell shocked, like he didn't know what to do. "Don't let anyone near her until tomorrow night."

Perfect. That gave him complete permission to hide Heli away from everyone and no one would question why he didn't rejoin the party. If he could figure out how, he was getting her the fuck out of here. Kosta gave Decker a small salute, made eye contact with Teagan and then threw Heli up and over his shoulder like the Neanderthal he was feeling like.

Heli squealed but kept her mouth shut. He hoped she knew that was a narrow escape. He marched her up the stairs, right past Mariya who was sitting on the top stair out of sight. "I hope you know what you're doing, boy."

He didn't. Kosta was through planning and plotting, trying to prove himself to anyone and everyone. He was operating on pure instinct now.

The door to her room was open a crack, so he kicked it, pushed through, and slammed it shut behind them. All the locks in this shithole were broken, so he grabbed the lone chair and jammed it under the door knob. No one was coming into this room without his say so.

Satisfied they were semi-secure, he tossed Heli down on the bed. He'd love to paddle her ass, and one of these days he would, but not today. Today he had something much more important to do.

Kosta crawled up over Heli, surprised she hadn't said anything or protested his treatment of her yet. It spoke to how scared she had been by what took place a minute ago that she was still silent. He wanted to wipe all that fear from her. His wolf howled inside that she should never be scared.

Enough was enough. No more pretending, no more play acting. No more. "Heli. You need to know that I won't ever let that man or any other mark and claim you."

She swallowed and her eyes were as wide as a bunny caught in a predator's trap. "You won't?"

"No." He pulled at the collar of the shitty white dress and it ripped away like tissue paper. He did it again with the sleeve baring her neck and shoulder. "Do you know why I can't let that happen?"

Heli licked her lips and then grabbed the other sleeve of the dress and yanked it off. She tossed the material to the floor and took a deep breath. The buttons holding the remaining fabric across her chest popped off and flew across the room. The material fell open baring the prettiest lacy bra covering her breasts. "Because of crazy-girl's prophecy? I think that might have been a real one. She was different this time."

Kosta lowered his lips and kissed her in the sensitive spot behind her ear. Then he whispered, low and harsh. "Because you are mine. Do you hear me? Mine."

She stilled and he lifted his head to see her reaction. Her mouth formed an O, but sound didn't come out. She blinked a few times and found her voice. "What about–"

"Fuck Violet's prophecy, real or fake" he tore the rest of the dress open, "and fuck Decker," she helped him shred the skirt of the stupid poofy thing, "and fuck the new moon."

Now there was only her lacy bra and her adorable pink underpants decorated with bunny rabbits between them. The undergarments weren't going to last long. Kosta shoved the bra strap aside and licked Heli from her shoulder to the beating pulse in her neck. He followed the same path back, dragging his teeth across her skin until he found exactly the right spot. "I am marking and claiming you tonight so no other wolf can ever lay a hand on you."

Heli exposed her neck and grabbed his head in her hands, holding his mouth to her sweet skin. "Finally."

MINE

It's not like she and Kosta hadn't done all the fun sexy times. They were great in bed together and always burned up the sheets. There was something very different about what was happening between them right now.

This wasn't sex. This wasn't screwing, or even fucking.

Yeah, he'd ripped off that horrid dress they'd shoved her into and there was a feverish roughness about the way he was touching and kissing her. But this wasn't about lust. What she saw in Kosta's eyes reflected what had been building in her heart for him for a long time.

This was love.

Frantic love.

With every lick, suck, and nip of her skin, he whispered, "mine, mine, mine." He claimed each part of her from her eyelids to her throat to the tops of her breasts. He slipped a hand behind her and unclasped her bra, shoving the thing down her arms and chest. He licked one nipple and then the other.

"Yes, Kosta. I'm yours. Make me yours." She wrapped her legs around his waist and pressed her center against him. Damn these clothes. Why was he still dressed?"

She grabbed for the hem of the t-shirt he was wearing and pulled it up his back, yanking to get it off of him. It had been a hundred million years since she'd run her hands over his chest and muscled abs. She was going to lick her way down that six-pack and keep going until she had her lips wrapped around his long, hard, luscious cock.

Kosta jerked the shirt over his head and it joined the shreds of dress on the floor. "I'm sorry we didn't do this before. I'm so sorry I got you into this mess because I didn't claim you and protect you the way a mate should."

Mate. She was going to be his mate. Simply thinking the word in her head had warmth radiating throughout her body, like she was fevered in all the right ways.

A month ago this word hadn't meant anything more to her than any other in the English language. Now, it was her life's blood. Being his mate meant everything. If she wasn't so happy and hot for him, she'd cry. "None of that matters. Only what we do now and for the rest of our lives together."

"I swear I will do my best to keep you safe. We're in one hell of a mess here, *zaika*. We shouldn't even be up here together. My need for you is putting us both in danger." There was so much regret in his voice that it hurt her heart.

She cupped his cheek and gave him a soft kiss. "We'll figure that out together. Later. Right now you need to take your pants off and–"

She didn't even finish her sentence before he rolled over, shucked his jeans and was back. "You're the one with too many clothes on now."

Heli ran her fingers down one side of his abs and up the other. He was so damn good looking. "Yes, I am."

She lost herself in his body for a moment until she felt his hands tugging at her panties. "Don't you even think about ripping those off me. They are the only undies I have and I've been washing them out every morning so I could keep wearing them. I am not going around pantyless."

He got a sly smile on his face. "When we figure out how to get the fuck out of this catastrophe and get back home, you are always going around without panties."

"You're naughty." She giggled and it felt so good she did it again. Earlier today she wasn't sure she was ever going to get the chance to smile again, and now she couldn't stop. "I am not."

They'd been given a reprieve, by Violet of all people, and she was going to take a hold of every morsel of happiness while she could.

"You definitely are because if you even think about covering this pussy with any kind of panties, they'll be shredded faster than that dress." He ran his fingers along the edge and gave them a tug. "Now lift your ass so I can pull them down, or you will lose them forever."

She squeaked and lifted her bum. Kosta pulled her

panties down with his thumbs, but spread his hands wide, caressing every inch of skin from her butt all the way down her thighs, and tickled the back of her knees, before her panties joined the rest of their clothes on the floor. Kosta kissed his way back up her leg, nibbling and teasing her as he got closer and closer to her pussy.

He licked the inside of her thigh. "God, I love the taste of you. You're already so wet for me. I don't understand how no one else has been tempted by your sweet scent."

"Wait." He swiped his tongue right over her clit. "Oh, god. No don't wait. Do that again. But you can smell that?"

He chuckled and did indeed lick her again. "I can always smell your lust and desire for me, love. It makes me so fucking hot for you, knowing you want me like I want you."

"I knew that, and Mariya warned me any kind of scent of sex would drive the wolves all crazy. So I've been using the no smell spray your mom gave me, you know, down there." She waved her hand indicating the space his head was currently occupying.

Kosta popped his head up. "No smell spray? From my mom?"

A lock of his hair had fallen into his eyes and he was so sexy with his head between her legs like that. "Yeah, it's like the opposite of perfume."

"Well, it isn't working. You still smell like brown sugar and butter and..." he tipped his head to the side and thought for a second, "ripe peaches soaked in honey and vanilla."

Wow. "That's awfully specific. You just kind of taste, umm, salty."

He grinned at her. "My senses are more highly attuned than yours."

She stuck her tongue out at him. "I have a highly refined palette, I'll have you know."

Kosta's face became serious and he pushed himself up on his hands and knees. He moved out from between her legs and lay beside her, head propped up on one arm. He touched the spot on her shoulder where he'd scraped his teeth earlier, swirling his fingers around and around in a circle, "If I mark you and you develop the ability to shift into a wolf like Gal did, you'll see what I mean."

Gosh. She hadn't actually connected those two things in her mind. This werewolf thing was still in that strange phase between a fairy tale and reality. She didn't know what was real and what wasn't. Heli knew her friend had developed the ability to shift, but not the how or why. Violet had also been marked by Decker and she had some pseudo psychic abilities. The mark was apparently the spark that made things happen. "I don't really get how all this works, you know. Do you think I will turn into a werewolf?"

"You did get dragged into my world pretty abruptly and I wish I could do this all over again. The truth is, I don't know. Until Maxy and Gal, wolves didn't mate humans. I don't think anyone is sure what all the effects and consequences are or will be. There aren't any rules or rituals that go with taking a human as a mate. " He seemed to be apologizing, but then a flash went through his eyes and he lit up with a smile.

He bolted off the bed and rooted around the room, looking for something. He grabbed her bag off the lone little desk and dumped it out. "Aha."

He lifted an open bag of really old chocolate covered pretzels she'd completely forgotten were in there. Strange thing to get excited about. "If you need a snack, I can knock on Mariya's door. She probably still has some madeleines left."

Kosta rooted through the plastic bag and pulled a pretzel out that had lost its criss-cross insides and was now a sad lumpy oval. "Perfect."

Not really. Where was he going with this? Chocolate covered pretzels were one of the world's most perfect snack foods, salty and sweet, just like her and Kosta. Aww.

She doubted his mind had come up with the same analogy. Guys' brains didn't do stuff like that.

He dragged her up off the bed and then to her complete surprise, went down on one knee. Sunbursts popped into her vision and a butterfly took up residence in her chest where her heart was supposed to be. "What are you doing?"

"Heli, I haven't done things right with you from the beginning. I'm not even doing this right, but I'm trying." He looked at her with that gorgeous smile, the swirl of purple in his eyes, and so much love that the whole room swelled with it. Or maybe that was just her heart.

"I swear to spend the rest of my life making you happy if you'll let me. I don't know what's going to happen when I mark you and make you mine, and I can't wait to find out. I want you to be my mate and I want you to be my wife. Will you mate and marry me?" He held out the pretzel like the most precious of engagement rings, picked a tiny bit of fuzz off of it and gave her a lopsided grin. "I promise if we live through the next few days, I'll buy you the biggest and most beautiful ring in the world."

Her throat squeezed with all the emotions bubbling up and out of her soul for him. She laughed and nodded and cried to shake them all out. "I don't care if you put a chicken nugget, or a donut hole, or an onion ring on my finger. I just want to spend the rest of my life with you. Yes, I'll marry you and mate you and all the other m-words we can think of that mean being together."

Kosta slid the chocolate pretzel onto her finger and she didn't even wait for it to go all the way on before she pulled him up to kiss him forever and ever. They slid back down onto the bed and wrapped themselves around each other.

Heli couldn't get enough touching and tasting him. "Please, Kosta. I need you now. I want you inside of me."

"Fuck, yes, baby." He pressed his thigh between her legs and spread her knees open. "We didn't get far in the foreplay, are you ready for me?

"Silly wolf, don't you know, I'm always wet for you." She grabbed his hand and moved it between their bodies, down to her pussy.

Kosta groaned when his fingers reached her slick folds. He spread her wet heat around, pressing his thumb against her clit and sliding two fingers inside of her. "I want to make this so good for you. I want you coming on my cock a half dozen times before I fill you with my seed."

"Keep talking like that, and doing that with your hands, and I'm going to come before you even get inside of me."

"Yes. Let me see you come for me. I want you even wetter before I fuck you." He swirled his thumb and wiggled his fingers, pushing her body toward orgasm. "That's it. I can feel your pussy squeezing my fingers. It's going to feel so god-damned good when I get inside of you."

She gripped the sheets on either side and groaned. They'd never been quiet but she couldn't exactly scream his name, not with a bunch of cranky wolves downstairs. She bit her lip to keep from crying out and whimpered.

Kosta pressed his lips to her ear. "That's it, love. Come on, give it to me. Let go and come for me."

She closed her eyes and gasped, letting the orgasm take her and trying to swallow her cries. Stars swam behind her eyelids and turned into rainbows of shimmering light as her body flooded with pleasure.

"You're so fucking beautiful when you come." Kosta whispered so only she could hear. "So fucking beautiful all the damn time. I don't know how the hell I got so lucky to be with you."

That had to be orgasm brain talking because she was the one who was lucky to be with him. She'd tell him so just as soon as she caught her breath.

Kosta rubbed his beard-rough face along the crease of her neck and her shoulder, then kissed along the same path. "You'll make a gorgeous wolf if you do shift, but even if you don't I think you will develop some kind of ability. Decker was wrong about only true alphas being able to give a human an ability with their mark. The Troikas have a dozen mates with abilities now. I know it's a bit late to ask, but are you going to be okay with that?"

"Uh, yeah. That's flipping cool as all get out. What exactly do you have to do to mark me? Gal said something about biting? That's kinda hot."

Kosta licked his lips and she noticed his wolf fangs had dropped. "I've been trying like hell not to bite you for weeks. The wolf inside of me has pushed and prodded me to mark you and it's all I can do to keep it contained now."

"Then don't. I want you, all of you. Bite me, Kosta. Wait, I don't mean it like that." She giggled. "I want you to bite and mark me."

He kissed the tip of her nose. "I know, *zaika*."

His hips pressed against hers and he notched his cock at the entrance to her pussy. "I love you, Heli. More than I thought possible. I love you."

Heli wrapped her legs around the back of his. Kosta thrust inside of her, pushing in as deep as he could go, filling her so perfectly. "I love you, too. Make me yours."

Kosta buried his face in the crook of her neck and set up a fast, hard rhythm, plunging his cock into her over and over. "Heli, you feel so fucking good. I'm not going to last much longer. God, your cunt is gripping me so tight."

He was right. As much as they'd had sex, she thought she knew what he felt like inside of her, but this was different. Better than ever before. "Don't stop. Don't even slow down."

Kosta growled low and deep and nipped at the skin of her neck. Contrary to what she'd just said he did slow down and stop. "Roll over. I need... fuck, I need you–"

He didn't finish what he was saying before he had her hips in his hands and was turning her over. His palm caressed her ass and pulled her tight against his groin, and shoved his cock back inside her pussy with another growl.

Okay, doggy-style it was then. She loved this position just as much as the next girl, especially since she could reach between her legs and rub her clit in time to his thrusts. She moved to do exactly that, but Kosta slapped her hand out of the way.

"Mine." He pulled her up so they were both kneeling and grabbed the insides of her thighs, spreading them open. His hand delved between her legs and found her clit. He pinched the tight nub and flicked his fingers over and over and over.

With his cock fucking into her from behind and his fingers flying over her clit, the tension built inside of her like the force of a tidal wave. "Kosta, please. Oh god, yes. Yes."

He nudged her head aside with his own and licked across the taut muscle between her neck and shoulder. The scrape of his teeth stung for a second before he bit down hard, burying his wolf's fangs into her skin. The pleasure and pain sent her skyrocketing into a climax. She cried out his name and Kosta covered her mouth with his other hand stifling her sounds of pleasure.

He pounded between her legs animalistically and his cock seemed to grow even more with each thrust. He grunted, and on a long groan, sunk in deeper than ever before. Heli felt the hot spurts of his seed in her channel and her pussy clenched around him as if milking every bit of his cum from his body.

The stars she'd seen with her earlier orgasm flashed again as if she were being propelled through space. While her body relaxed, her mind floated in this beautiful, warm sparkling light. If she opened her mind to the light, she knew she could see more, but something or someone was pulling her back.

Kosta. He was softly calling her name. *Heli, Heli, all mine. Finally mine. Heli.*

Her mind floated back into her body. Kosta was still buried inside of her pussy. It was as if he were locked inside of her and she loved the feeling. Gently he released her mouth and pulled his fingers from her pussy. He lowered them both down to the bed and hugged her body close. They were both breathing hard and Heli didn't want to ever move again. She pulled the blanket over them and basked in Kosta's heat surrounding her from the inside out.

He softly swiped his tongue over the place where he'd bit her and tingles spread across her skin there. "You'll have a bruise at first, but slowly it will turn into my mark. Anyone who looks at you will know you belong to me, and me to you."

"I can't wait to see it." They snuggled close and she drifted for a few moments reliving every second of their joining. She'd never seen him quite so out of control, but in control of her and her body this way. She felt like, for the first time, he'd let the real Konstantin come out to play. "You still feel so big inside of me."

He held her even tighter than before and kissed the area around her neck. "It's the wolf's knot, our bodies are locked together until my wolf is satisfied your cunt is mine and mine alone."

"I'm pretty sure I'm not supposed to think that's hot, but I do."

"I'm glad you think so, because it's probably going to happen all of the time now that you're mine. At least until you're pregnant."

She closed her eyes and saw little lilac-eyed children running along a beach. They would be so adorable.

"Heli?"

The soft vision in her mind changed and Heli saw her sister, dressed in flowing white robes, the wind whipping through her hair, wearing a crown. Zara was standing right outside on the front lawn of the Bay hotel. Heli reached out to touch her, but there was nothing there. Zara looked directly at her and said, "The Crescent moon is rising over the Bay. Be careful."

The voice from before, that had called her back from the starry, starry night, said her name again. *Heli, my little bunny, come back to me, love.*

She opened her eyes and looked right into Kosta's. They

weren't purple like she expected them to be, but still that dark blue with the purple swirls.

"Heli? Are you okay?" There was a tone of fear in his voice.

"Sweetheart. I don't think I'm going to get the ability to shift into a wolf. I think you gave me the ability to see the future."

PRETTY PINK VISIONS

Kosta hadn't known he could be both deliriously happy and scared out of his freaking skull at the same time. Heli had agreed to be his mate and his wife, but until he could find a way for them to escape the watchful eye of Decker and Teagan, she was in serious danger.

He'd already thwarted several attempts by both of them to check in on Heli. Thanks to her no-smell perfume, the smell of sex that should have tipped everyone off to their illicit affairs was defunct. After the first time he turned them away, Heli came up with a plan to make it look like he'd tied her to a chair so she couldn't get away. She recruited Mariya to help and that seemed to satisfy both the alphas.

There was only a few more hours until the darkest part of the darkest night of the month. The new moon could suck his dick for taking so damn long to get here. Why

Violet's vision had to specify tonight, when wolves were at their weakest, made him suspicious. Kosta might have suspected she'd found out about his plans for the packs to attack last night, except Heli swore she thought Vi's vision was a real one.

He wasn't so sure. It was awfully convenient that her prophecy made it so Decker couldn't screw around with any other women. That vision was completely self serving for her, except for the fact that it only kept him away from Heli for one night. If she'd faked it, wouldn't she have set it up so Decker's dick would shrink off if he touched any woman but her?

Regardless, it gave him the time to figure out how the hell to get Heli to safety in the face of this enormous clusterfuck. Kosta was ready to throw her over his shoulder and drag her back to Troika territory and give up all his plans to destroy the Bay pack. She absolutely wouldn't go.

She wanted to wait for Zara. Both Mariya's contacts and Heli's vision said Zara and Crescent pack were coming here tonight. Since Kosta's plans to get rid of Bay last night hadn't worked, they were caught in the middle. Ramsey Crescent wouldn't destroy and dismantle the Bay pack. He'd take them over as his own.

It was a brilliant strategic move. With Ramsey's own territory to the north, and taking over Bay and Fire Island to the south, Crescent would be flanking Troika territory. It wouldn't be long before he'd close in on Max and the rest of Kosta's friends and family.

Kosta couldn't let that happen. He had to stay and fight

off Ramsey. He had to take Decker's one-blood reign of terror down. He couldn't do either of those and keep Heli safe.

He needed help and he needed it quick. He had no idea if his brother would respond since he still thought Kosta had betrayed the Troika pack. Max had sent several more texts that consisted mostly of one word. Fuck. He blamed Kosta for the death of the Fire Island alpha too.

He had to try.

Max, Heli and I are in trouble. May not survive the night. Send help.

The reply came back right away.

Fuck off you fucktard. Why don't you ask Niko?

What the hell did that mean? Niko was barely functioning, he wouldn't be able to help get Heli to safety. Kosta considered sending a reply back begging, but he doubted he'd get anything back except for more name calling. He only had one more person to ask.

He would spend the rest of his days with his tail between his legs, begging, if it would save Heli. He started typing the text to his mother.

Her number popped up on his screen before he even got the first word typed out.

Tell Mariya to hide the milk. We're coming for tea.

Kosta had no idea what that meant, but he was smart enough to do as his mother told him. He knocked on Mariya's door and poked his face in. She and Heli had their heads bent over some kind of project. "Heli. I have to go down soon. If I beg you, will you stay hidden or try to escape?"

"No, love. Zara will be here soon."

Sigh. He didn't think so, but it was worth asking. What he couldn't tell her was that he wasn't leaving that decision in her hands. His last hope, his only one now to keep her safe, was to betray her too. He'd made arrangements with Mariya and the few wolves left that were loyal to her and not Decker to lead Heli away from danger.

They would tell her they'd made contact with Zara and that she was waiting for them to come to her. Mariya and the good wolves would take Heli to Selena at the Troika pack house and ask for asylum. All while Kosta burned down the world to make it a better place for her to live in.

Without him.

He couldn't see a way he would survive the night. Not when he had to kill both Decker and Ramsey and without declaring himself alpha of either pack, the remaining pack members would kill him.

"Troika." Decker's angry growl of his name surged up the stairs.

"That's my cue. Gotta go. Come here and kiss me for luck." Kiss me for the last time.

Heli smiled at him and crossed the room. She gave him a long sensuous kiss. It promised more and he hated to miss it. He was going to fucking try hard to live through the night so he could get back to her. But he was glad he'd made the right kind of arrangements with Mariya in case he didn't make it.

"Troika," Decker bellowed again.

"Love you, *zaika*."

"Love you, too."

He would carry those words to his grave whether that be tonight or a hundred years from now. "Oh and tell Mariya, my mother said to hide the milk because she's coming for tea. I assume you two know what that means."

"Oh gosh. She did, she is? I'd better get ready." Heli kissed him again quickly. "Be safe."

He made sure the door was shut tight and heard her slip the chair under the doorknob before he turned and made his way down the stairs. The sun had set hours ago and all the wolves of the five packs had gathered to see who would mark and claim Heli.

Ha. They wouldn't get the satisfaction. Bastards.

Decker pointed to Kosta as he walked into the crowd. "I trusted you, Troika, as did all of these alphas here under the new moon. Think you can take over my pack? Think again."

So it was going to go that way. Fine. "I don't want your pathetic pack of one-bloods, Decker. I want it destroyed. You and your kind taint the good name of wolves around the world. These alphas aren't here to join with you, they agreed to come here and wipe you and your kind from history."

The five alphas stepped forward, even Teagan who addressed Decker. "We've seen enough in one night to know Troika is right. Prepare for your end, Decker."

Decker didn't even flinch. He grabbed Violet from

where she was sitting at his feet and thrust her toward the crowd. "Tell all these pack leaders what you saw."

Violet looked around at the room wide-eyed. She clearly hadn't known he was going to call her out. She walked up to Decker's chair and he turned her to face the audience. He bent and whispered something to her and she nodded, then spoke. "You all heard my prophecy yesterday and saw Decker's intention to claim the catalyst tonight. I foresaw that if the wrong wolf claimed her, this pack would be destroyed. But I didn't understand until today, it wouldn't be just our pack. Everyone who bore witness to the prophecy will be destroyed. Each of you and your packs will–"

The crowd erupted into angry shouts and concern. Kosta didn't move. This was another play by Violet. She must have found out about him and Heli, or Decker had and was coercing her into saying all of this. Fucking hell.

Decker held up his hand to quiet the room.

Violet looked directly at Kosta just as Decker had a moment ago. A shiver rolled through his body. She held out her arms and pointed directly at him. "Konstantin Troika has betrayed you all. He marked and claimed the catalyst for himself hoping for greatness."

Kosta heard a squeak from the top of the staircase behind him. Fuck. Heli had left the safety of Mariya's room. God, no. Don't let her reveal herself. There were too many wolves here who didn't know the truth from the trees. He couldn't keep her safe from them all.

Heli's scent hit him before he turned and saw her

floating down the stairs in a new and improved version of that ugly dress from yesterday. She looked perfect, gorgeous and ethereal. She stood at the top of the landing and pointed at Violet. "You're a liar."

Fuck. "Heli. Don't. Stay back."

She looked at him and begged him with her eyes not to say anything more. She descended down the stairs like a ghost. "I know she lies, because I too have the power to see the future. But my gift is not unreliable like Violet's, nor do I fake my visions to get what I want. I bear the mark of a true alpha where she does not."

Teagan and his men stopped Heli as she got to the bottom of the steps. "Show us, woman. Have you been marked and claimed by Kosta?"

"I will proudly show you my mark. I belong to Kosta and he belongs to me." She tugged the neck of her t-shirt aside and bared a glowing purple moon with black wolf in the center tattooed on her skin.

Teagan stared down at Heli's mark and then shoved her aside. He stalked toward Kosta, the gray glow of his wolf in his eyes.

Kosta let his wolf rise up at the new threat Teagan presented. His claws came out and his vision changed from man to beast. "Touch my mate again and I will destroy you."

Teagan didn't back down for a second. "You son of a bitch. No better than your power hungry brothers. We all saw that witch's vision last night. We don't know that your Heli has any kind of powers at all. But since you've marked her, the path of the prophecy has been chosen. You've doomed us all with your greed."

"Shut up, both of you," Decker shouted. "There's more. Violet is a true seer and she has seen our fates."

Violet swallowed hard and nodded. "All is not lost. He is the only man who can save you now. He who betrayed us must change his own path and in turn, will change all of yours."

Teagan growled. "How? He's already marked the catalyst for his own greed. How can he possibly change that path now? I say we kill him. If he and this woman he marked are dead, nothing will come of it."

"She is my mate, Teagan. You'd do well to remember that." This asshole just went to the top of Kosta's list of who to kill tonight. Might as well get one out of the way.

Decker pushed Violet aside and stepped between Kosta and Teagan. "No. You can't just kill him. He has to prove to us all he isn't like this brother and after the throne himself. It's his greed that is our undoing. It's the greed of all the Troikas that's brought this pack war upon us. We must destroy the Troikas before their tangled web of doing whatever the fuck they want spreads like a plague among all of wolfkind."

Oh, because Decker was one to talk. He wanted to be the new wolf Tzar more than anyone here, and Kosta was about to point that out, but Decker wouldn't shut up. He talked over them all.

"Here's how he can change his path and all of ours." Decker waved his hand over his head and a battered and beaten group of Bay enforcers struggled to bring in a man, dirty and naked, and threw him to the floor. He immediately got to his feet and howled with a dark and creepy sound that sent a chill through everyone in the room, making them all shiver at the sound.

That chill hit Kosta the hardest and shook him all the way to his core. "Niko?"

Niko turned and snarled at Kosta, stalking around him like he was easy prey and Niko was going to eat him up.

The rest of the wolves and women formed a circle around Kosta and Niko, giving them a wide berth. In the fray, Decker grabbed Heli by the hair and held her tight against his chest. She fought him like a banshee, until he shifted his hand and arm into the wolf's paw and claw and pressed it to her throat.

Kosta lunged for Decker, but Niko snarled and caught his arm, throwing him to the floor.

Decker laughed while the rest of the audience watched in horror. "Kill him, Kosta or he'll kill you. Show us you aren't a part of the Troika conspiracy to take over the throne and I'll let you and your mate live in my pack. But I warn you, if you let your brother kill you, Heli dies too."

"You douche nozzle, let me go." Heli squirmed, but Decker only held her tighter against his chest.

"Don't move, you whore. I should have taken you when I had the chance." Decker pressed his claw into Heli's throat and a dribble of blood seeped down her skin.

The red of her blood turned Kosta's vision red too. His wolf rose up and without conscious thought his bones and skin cracked, his clothes shredded in a burst and he transformed into the great black wolf. His growl was deep and loud enough that the light bulbs in the room shook and shattered over their heads. More than half the men in the room also shifted into wolves in response to Kosta's growled warning and many scattered, except those loyal to Decker or Teagan.

Kosta's muscles bunched, ready to attack the still human form of Decker, but the asshole held Heli's life in his hands. There was no way to hurt Decker without also hurting Heli.

Brother.

Niko's voice, tired and broken, popped into Kosta's head.

Kosta whipped around expecting to see the white wolf of his brother, but saw only the man. In their human forms, they could not speak into each other's minds. Only mates could communicate in mixed forms this way and Niko was not his mate. This didn't make sense.

Kill me, Niko said.

Kosta's chest constricted until he couldn't breath. Surely he hadn't heard Niko correctly. He must mean that they should kill Decker. He tried to mindspeak back to Niko, but nothing happened. He shook his great furry head to tell his brother no fucking way.

Konstantin, you must kill me. Kill me and save your mate. At least that sacrifice will mean something in this world.

Niko closed his eyes, let his head fall back, and spread his arms out, opening himself up for the attack.

"Kill him, Kosta, or your mate dies and I kill your brother for you." Decker snarled and Heli squeaked in pain.

"Wait. Don't anyone move. I'm having a vision," Heli yelled. The room was almost completely black with no moon to shine in the windows and no light bulbs over head. Suddenly a bright flash of electricity arced through the air around her.

Decker fell to the floor, shaking and convulsing as the electricity poured from Heli to him. Heli shouted, "I foresee that Decker pees himself and that the Crescent pack are on their way here. If you don't want to die, you should all bolt."

She snorted at her own little joke and sent one more surge of electricity into Decker's body on the floor. The scent of urine filled Kosta's nostrils and he knew Heli's first prediction was coming true.

Wolves and women went every which way, but Kosta made a path through them all directly toward his mate. He was big enough that his head was just about even with her face. So he licked her.

"Oh my God. Kosta that had better be you. I can't see a thing."

It is, zaika. *Drop your taser and let's get Niko.*

"Yeah, good idea."

The front door of the hotel blew open and a woman in white so bright she lit up the room walked in. "Hold."

Every man, woman, and wolf in within the sound of her voice instantly froze. Kosta couldn't move, couldn't shift, could barely think. A very powerful force was holding them all perfectly still and there was no breaking it.

"Rise, Decker Kosatka, alpha of Bay and Fire Island and hear the challenge."

Decker's body rose into the air and while he wasn't dead, he wasn't all there either. His head wobbled to the side, but he was breathing, and his eyes were open. Slurred words came out of his mouth. "State your challenge, emissary."

These were old phrases, used long ago, before the Volkovs reigned and packs challenged each other in never ending wars.

"Ramsey Crescent, alpha of the Crescent, Fall River, Pachaug, and Burlingame packs challenges you and all others present for your fealty. Show your throats or die this first night of the new moon."

A big gray and silver wolf pushed into the room and howled. With that sound, they all got their freedom from the power holding them and Heli ran across the room. "Zara!"

ALPHA WHO?

Zara was alive, and glowing. Like literally, and Heli didn't care if Zara was radioactive. Finally she could hug her big sister once again, which is what she was doing. Only Zara wasn't hugging her back. She just stood there, stiff as a wax museum figure of herself.

"Zara?"

A great big grey and silver wolf pushed past her and then transformed into a man. He looked over at Heli and raised one eyebrow like she was something interesting, but insignificant. He surveyed the room like he owned it and that it wasn't up to his standards.

"Who are the alphas here? Decker? Where are you, you little rat?"

Okay, at least he recognized that Decker was a douche. He must have something going on up in his noggin. Heli decided that meant she could risk drawing a little attention to herself and pointed to Decker. "He's that guy, there. The one who peed his pants when I tased him."

The other eyebrow raised up when he looked at her this time and she felt a bit more significant. So far so good. She took Zara's hand in hers and tried to get her to cross the room with her. Zara didn't budge. Most everyone else was still sort of frozen, but not because of that crazy power unleashed on them. They all seemed too intimidated to move.

Maybe Heli should take that as a hint. But you know what? She was fucking done with these alpha werewolves and their bullshit. She'd tased one and she'd do it again if she had to. Except she'd used up the one jolt she had on douchepotato king. Fine, then she'd kick anyone who gave her any guff in the nuts.

She patted Zara's hand. "I'll be right back, okay. I just want to make sure Kosta is okay."

Zara didn't say anything or even look at her. That wasn't good. One thing at a time. Heli followed the path silver wolf dude had taken, then veered to Kosta. He was still in his wolf form and was watching silver dude's every move.

"Hey, baby. Who is that?" she whispered.

Ramsey Crescent, the alpha of a rival pack. He is the one who took your sister.

"What? That bastard. I'm gonna give him a–"

Ramsey looked back at her and Kosta stepped between them. *Zaika. Calm yourself. Ramsey is a very powerful alpha and would make a better ally than an enemy.*

"You want me to make friends with the guy that kidnapped my sister and turned her into that?"

"Hush, woman," Ramsey snarled.

Kosta growled at Ramsey, but spoke gently into her mind. *No, love. I don't want you to provoke him. If we're going to get out of this alive and with our siblings, we need to be very careful.*

"Fine." She gave Ramsey the middle finger to his back after he turned to face Decker. That was all the concession she was willing to give at this point.

Ramsey put a hand on Decker's shoulder and pushed him to his knees on the ground. "Show your throat and yield your pack to me or shift and fight for the right to lead them."

The wet spot at the front of Decker's pants grew bigger and he tilted his head back exposing his throat to Ramsey.

"Good," Ramsey said and then slashed Decker's throat, taking his head clean off with his claws. The head flew across the room and smashed into the old cuckoo clock on the wall. The poor bird made a horrible death knell as wood and metal went flying everywhere. "You were a pathetic excuse for a wolf and no alpha. I don't stand with one-bloods."

Holy crap. Heli didn't know whether to clap or cry. Decker deserved to die, but Kosta wasn't kidding when he warned her not to make enemies with this guy.

Ramsey shifted his arm back to human and calmly wiped the blood from his hands on Decker's former throne. "Anyone else anxious to spout the stupidity of the one-blood dogma? I will happily help you join your alpha. Otherwise, show your throats and pledge your fealty to me as the new alpha of Bay pack."

No one said a thing, but all the Bay enforcers that Heli recognized got down on their knees and exposed their throats to him. Ramsey looked around the room and spotted Teagan who wasn't cowering quite as much as the others, and wasn't showing his throat. "Teagan of Chincoteague. What are you doing consorting with the likes of the Bay pack? I have always heard you and your family were good leaders."

Teagan stood. "We are. The other alphas and I came here to do the same as you. To end Decker's reign of terror."

Ramsey nodded. "Not quite the same as me, though. I'm here to take over the pack, and now that includes yours."

Teagan took a step back. "We have no grievance with you."

"Nevertheless, you were included in the challenge my emissary gave." Ramsey indicated to Zara who hadn't moved from her spot.

Teagan glared over at Kosta, but got down on one knee and lifted his head. "Chincoteague pack pledges its fealty to you, Ramsey, alpha of the Crescent pack."

Ramsey put a hand on Teagan's shoulder and the room took a collective sigh of relief that no more heads were rolling around the room. "Now, let's see who else is here. I know I smelled more than one Troika, and we have old debts to be settled, don't we? Where is your alpha, little Kosta?"

Kosta growled and maneuvered so his body blocked Ramsey from Heli and Niko. He didn't shift or show Ramsey his throat. A showdown was about to happen between the two of them.

Heli'd had enough of that. She popped her head over Kosta's big furry shoulder. "No other Troikas here. It's just us, so feel free to move on to your next fealty swearing in ceremony. I think you missed that guy over there."

Ramsey narrowed his eyes at her. "Interesting. I heard the Troikas were progressive, but I had no idea they let their women speak for them."

Kosta growled some more and bared his teeth at Ramsey. Heli whispered to him, "Yeah, you tell him, babe."

Ramsey wasn't even a little bit intimidated. "You are going to make a perfect mate for my Taryn, little Troika. She's been all moony-eyed over you for a long time. But she doesn't do well with authority. If you're all good with letting your woman be in charge, you and Taryn will get along just fine."

Exsqueeze me? "Sorry, that's a no go. Kosta can't hook up with your daughter. He's already mated to me."

Heli. Do not interfere. I will not be mating Taryn Crescent. She doesn't even like me.

Ramsey crossed the room so fast that Heli didn't even see him move. His wolves attacked Kosta, pushing and shoving him away from Heli. She was face to face with Ramsey without her wolf to protect her. He sniffed her like a weird creepy pervert. "Good try, little girl, but his scent isn't on you. Nor do I sense a wolf in you. You are not mated and to claim you are deserves punishment. Shift, Kosta, and yield to me or I punish her here and now."

Kosta shifted into his human form and shoved the wolves around him aside. His eyes glowed with a blue so dark it was almost the purple she'd seen in her vision, and his wolf was not entirely gone from his form. "Don't you dare touch her."

Heli's heart was racing and this wolf-man would know that, but she was absolutely determined to keep her calm. Because if she lost it, her sister may be lost to her as well.

She didn't cower, move away, or even flinch in the face of the alpha-hole. No. Instead she glared up at him and held her hand up to halt Kosta's progress toward them. The hand with the still intact pretzel ring. Most of the chocolate had worn off, but she'd found some clear fingernail polish in Mariya's things and had shellacked the hell out of it.

"There hasn't been a full moon since we vowed to mate. Duh." At least she knew that much about becoming a mate in wolf culture. Plus, she had her mark, and the beautiful sign of their love for each other. She chose to display the ring for him instead of her mark. "I don't know what you do in your wolfy land, but see this ring, it means we're engaged."

Ramsey scoffed. "We don't recognize human ritual. Your promises are too weak."

"But mine is not. She. Is. Mine." Kosta placed his hand

on the back of her neck to show his claim on her and clasped her hand in his.

Ramsey's nostrils flared and Heli got that she was pushing on his last nerve. Her flippancy was her only armor though, so she put on another layer. She pushed up her eyebrow in an I-told-you-so quirk. "See."

"That we will. The full moon is in two weeks. You will be mated first in that ceremony in front of the entire rest of the pack. I relish seeing you submit on hands and knees, but it won't be to this Troika."

Ramsey raised his hand and his wolves bore down on them, snarling and growling. "You and your kin are too much trouble. I wouldn't have you in my pack even if you swore your fealty to me. You and your traitorous brother will die by my wolves' teeth tonight. We will be hailed by all of wolfkind for ending the two of you. Your brother's pack will be next."

Gulp. Time for Heli to kick those balls.

"Hold." Zara said the word loud and clear again. She moved forward through the frozen crowd and faced Ramsey. Her voice was as flat and emotionless as before. "This woman is also a seer. If you kill her mate before the full moon, her powers will not be fully realized."

Zara waved a hand and released Heli and Ramsey from her spell. Ramsey glanced between Heli and Zara. "How do you know she is a seer. I don't smell a mark on her and you haven't had a vision since we've been here."

"She is my sister."

Ramsey's jaw dropped open and he laughed. "Oh, that's

rich. But what do I need another seer for, when I have you?"

Zara didn't answer and Heli decided to think fast. "Because I've seen the future and I know who will become the next wolf Tzar."

For the first time tonight, Zara blinked and that seemed to break the spell on everyone in the room. She looked at Heli like she'd never seen her before in her life. Ramsey reached for Heli but met the wall of Kosta's bare chest instead. He jerked his hand back and let his claws burst out once again. "Tell me who, unless you want to watch your boy toy here die right now."

Well, poop on a poo poo platter.

"Touch Kosta and I'll never tell you. Move another inch and my lips will be sealed forever. Let them go and I will willingly tell you what I know." Heli stepped around Kosta and when he tried to stop her, she gave him a soft kiss to the corner of his mouth that said she knew what she was doing. He shook his head and pleaded with his eyes not to do this.

She had to. She would not let him die.

"I haven't seen it yet. I have seen that I will see it." Please buy that. It sounded better in her head than coming out of her mouth.

"Your sister can not lie to me, so I know what she says is true. You are a seer and that could come in handy. I will make you my mate at the full moon so your powers are fully realized and then you will not be able to lie to me either." Ramsey signaled to the wolves who closed in. Two grabbed Niko and yanked him down to the floor. Two more flanked her and Kosta, their mouths dripping in anticipation.

Kosta wouldn't be able to shift into a wolf in time.

Her threat to keep silent wasn't enough. She had to up the stakes. Heli bent to the ground and grabbed a jagged piece of metal that might have been half a gear from the internal workings of the dead cuckoo clock. She held the metal against the wound that Decker had already made in her throat. "I will die by my own hand before I let you kill Kosta or Niko."

"Heli. No," Kosta shouted.

Ramsey smiled. "You are a savvy opponent, Heli. You will be an asset to me. I concede. You can come with me now and serve me as a seer and I will spare Kosta and Niko, at least until our next battle. Beyond that I cannot guarantee their safety. I think you understand that."

She shook her head. "I will never willingly help you hurt them."

"I understand." Ramsey held his hand out for her pseudo weapon.

"Oh. Okay then." She handed over the piece of metal. "Umm. I guess I'll go with you."

"Good." He took her only weapon from her and tossed it far behind him. "Kosta, Niko. If I see either of you after the count of ten, all deals are off and Heli dies. One. Two. Three."

"Fuck you, Ramsey," Kosta spit out. "I won't leave Heli with you."

"Then all deals are off and your little girlfriend and you will both die right here, right now." Ramsey waved his hand. "Look around you, little Troika. You're surrounded. Even if you shift, you'll take out maybe one or two of my wolves and not before I slit Heli's throat. I don't need her, I just want her. Unlike you I can contain my impulses."

Heli's heart beat so fast she could barely get the words out. "Kosta, go. Please. I'll be alright."

Kosta narrowed his eyes. Then he shifted back into his black wolf. *I will come for you, Heli. I swear it.*

"Four. Five. Six. Better hurry boys. I don't think Niko is going to make it very far in the next four seconds."

Heli hadn't taken the time to look at Niko since the wolves had shoved him to the floor. They hadn't moved him from the spot where he'd opened his arms and waited for Kosta to kill him. He sat with his arms wrapped around his knees, blood pooling from the bite marks in his shoulders, staring up at Zara with tears running down his face.

Why hadn't he shifted to his wolf form too? Kosta wasn't going to be able to drag his brother away like that. "Ramsey, you have to give them a chance to get away. Ten seconds isn't long enough."

"Four more seconds is all they get." Ramsey signaled to the other men and wolves standing guard and they separated to give Kosta an escape route. "I've made it fair enough and given them every opportunity to get away. Seven. Eight."

From outside they heard the screech of tires coming to a fast halt in the dirt. Three big wolves crashed through the door with Gal right behind them. She pointed her hand at Ramsey and the Grimm wolves of her pack attacked.

The room erupted into total chaos and Heli dropped to the ground. She crawled toward Zara and yanked her down too. Zara blinked at her, and for the first time seemed to recognize Heli. She tipped her head to the side and the glow around her that had been lighting up the room went out like someone switched off her light.

Wolves snarled, claw and teeth clashed and a blood-curdling howl ripped through the air. Oh, God. She knew the sound of him. It was Kosta. He was hurt or worse.

"Kosta? Where are you?" She couldn't see anything except the headlights shining outside. She crawled toward the door, dragging Zara along with her. "Kosta, talk to me."

She tried again in her head, like he sometimes talked to her when he was in his wolf form. *Kosta. Please say something.*

Nothing. Please oh please oh please oh please don't let him be dead.

"Heli. Over here." A tiny light like from a pen light shined toward her and then at the floor, illuminating a path. At the end of that path, Violet was hiding behind Decker's old red recliner. "Come on."

Before Heli could even shake her head, someone or something grabbed Violet and dragged her out of sight. Crap. This was like a freaking horror movie. Didn't the cute blondes always die in horror movies? Heli refused to be too dumb to live. She kept moving toward the front door. Maybe if they could get out of the fray here Gal had more of her new pack outside that would protect them.

Yes, good plan. "Zara, let's get outside."

She didn't expect her sister to say anything, but suddenly Zara's hand was ripped from Heli's and Zara's scream turned Heli's blood to ice water. "No, Zara, Zara."

She couldn't lose Zara and Kosta.

She couldn't think like that. Kosta wasn't dead. He couldn't be. She'd know wouldn't she? That meant she needed to live too. To do that she had to get outside.

A wolf howl she didn't recognize sounded and something with a lot of sharp teeth grabbed Heli by the back of the shirt. She flailed, trying to get away, but it dragged her away, screaming. The beast shoved her into the waiting hands of someone else. She was knocked on the head, hard, and the last thing she heard as the blackness tunneled her vision was a chorus of howls.

ALPHA UP

Kosta knew only two things.

Heli was gone.

Ramsey Crescent was going to die.

The chaos of wolves fighting around him seeped through the filter of his pure rage. He didn't care even a little about which pack won, who killed whom, or why. He knew only that he was lost without the shining light of Heli.

He stalked through the battles, searching for the alpha, the one he would seek his revenge on. He would kill Ramsey for hurting Heli. He would eviscerate and defile his enemies corpses for even thinking he could take her as a mate.

Ramsey. Come out and fight me like a wolf, you coward. Stop hiding behind your enforcers.

Ramsey did not answer in words. Two Crescent wolves charged at Kosta in his stead. Kosta pulled upon every fighting skill his father had taught him and lashed out at the bellies of the beasts as they attacked. They were dead and lying at his feet in splashes of their own entrails before they could snap their jaws at him.

His answer came then.

You'll never see your girlfriend again, Kosta. She is mine now, as is her sister. The big silver wolf stepped into Kosta's path, his head low, and snarled. *I will rip their heads from their bodies for being abominations under the light of the moon. That is the punishment you and your brothers will get from me. You brought this anarchy down on us all by mating with humans and I will end it.*

The fighting around them died down as the rest of the wolves in the room recognized the battle royale that would determine their fates. Kosta had nothing and everything to lose. No pack, no family, no mate. His need to prove himself and his own egotistical decisions had lost him everything. Everything he'd ever needed in life, but couldn't see just how important they were to him.

He would give his life for them all if he had to.

Kosta didn't give his enemy any advantage and lunged at Ramsey, tearing a chunk of flesh and silver fur from his opponent. Ramsey was no newbie to the world of wolf fights. Kosta suffered a slash to his shoulder for starting the battle. First blood had been drawn by both.

I will take you apart piece by piece if I have to, Ramsey.

Ramsey circled looking for Kosta's weakness. *You can try. Even if you manage to kill me, I have an entire pack to avenge my death. You have no one and nothing. Your own brother has forsaken you for your betrayals and sent his weakling mate in his place. You can't even call yourself a Troika anymore.*

Those words hit Kosta harder than any physical strike Ramsey could have made. All of his plans had been for naught. He hadn't taken down the Bay pack, he'd only added to their numbers and practically handed them all over to the Crescents. His own brother, his alpha, hadn't even shown up in his hour of need because Kosta had done a great job making everyone think he was a one-blood.

The only person who believed in him was Heli and she wasn't here to help him believe in himself now. For the first time in his life, he had to either know who he was inside or not all on his own. No alpha, no father, no brothers to guide his path. He had to forge his way himself this time.

He could fight to his end and he would for Heli, but he knew deep down that he could never win. Because winning meant he would be the alpha of Crescent pack and he was many things, but he was no alpha.

He was a little brother, a rebel, a flirt. He was nothing more than a beta surrounded by alphas. How could he ever hope to beat a wolf who'd not only been raised to be an alpha, who commanded one of the largest and most powerful packs in the world?

If he allowed Ramsey to beat him, Gal and her Grimms were here. Even she had a better chance than he did. She was alpha in her own right and at least could avenge his death and go after Heli and Zara. She could probably even talk Max into the two of them challenging Ramsey for the Crescent pack themselves. Max had already proven in so many ways that he was a great leader.

Kosta was nothing but a screw up.

Heli would be better off without him. He'd already put her life in danger time and time again, just by being his usual fuck up self.

Kosta caught Ramsey bunching his muscles to strike again. His wolf wouldn't simply allow him to lay down and be killed, the fight response was too strong, but the man in him knew when to give up. He bared his teeth and let his wolf's instincts take over, but it wouldn't be enough.

Ramsey growled and charged, his teeth bared and aimed for Kosta's throat. Kosta slashed out with his claws in an effort to defend himself. He met flesh and drew blood, but not that of his opponent. The scent was too familiar and he recoiled at what he'd done.

The blood on his paws was Niko's.

Niko roared out his agony as Ramsey's jaws crushed down around his fragile human shoulder and chest. He thrust his human legs under the silver wolf's body and kicked hard, sending Ramsey flying across the room. Ramsey thudded against the wall, and shook his head like the sense was knocked out of him, but he wasn't injured and he didn't retreat. He wobbled a bit, but stared back toward Kosta and Niko with hatred in his eyes.

Brother. You must fight. Niko collapsed back onto the floor, blood pooling beneath him.

Niko, what have you done? Kosta stared at his brother, shocked, and didn't know what to do.

Niko grabbed the scruff of Kosta's neck and pulled him down, so they were face to face. *Nothing I haven't done before. Now quit being a dumbass and be the alpha.*

I'm not like you or Max. You were born to be alphas. You stand up and be one. Shift and heal. Shift and be the alpha we all know you are. The alpha we need.

Niko coughed and blood spurted out of his mouth. He was dying before Kosta's eyes. *I can't shift, I've lost my wolf. Besides, you too were born to be an alpha. All three of us were. Max has already taken his rightful place. Now it's your turn. You are an alpha. Try acting like one. All you need to do is get yourself a pack, and a powerful matriarch, dumbass.*

Niko closed his eyes and took a shuddering breath. Kosta howled and was joined in chorus by Gal's Grimm wolves. A new band of howls joined them from outside. Max in his great grey wolf form charged into the room. He took one look at Niko and Kosta and snarled.

Take this bastard's pack from him, little brother. I am behind you.

That same moment, Ramsey chose to attack.

Kosta lunged into the air to protect his brother, to be who he was meant to be. The two of them crashed into each other and tumbled to the ground in a mass of teeth, snarls, claws, and death. They slashed and bit and tore each other to pieces, but they were too evenly matched and neither was coming out on top.

Submit to me, Kosta. I am the alpha. Ramsey's alpha voice rang out trying to overpower the weaker wolf.

That wasn't Kosta anymore. He rammed his head into Ramsey's chest, pushing him to the ground. Kosta pounced, landing with his claws on Ramsey's throat. *I am the alpha now and this pack is mine.*

Ramsey whined and tried to get away, but Kosta held him tight. *I will concede the Bay pack to you, but never Crescent.*

You have no choice. Kosta pressed his claws into the fur and flesh of Ramsey's throat. He could hardly wait to rip Ramsey's head off as was his right.

Let me live and retreat and I will return the seers to you. Ramsey wiggled like one of the sturgeon from the Bay. *Kill me now and you'll never see them again.*

Kosta could so easily kill this piece of shit and claim the most powerful pack in the world. Crescent with it's alliances and claims on other packs was far stronger than anything the Troikas had ever claimed. With that kind of power, Kosta would be in line to be the new Wolf Tzar. And he didn't care even a little.

My mate is more important to me than your pack or you life. You may live, but if you ever threaten me or mine again, I will kill you and take your pack. Kosta shoved Ramsey away like the trash that he was. *Now shift and surrender.*

Ramsey shifted and held up his hands in surrender. "Taryn has your women and is probably long gone from here. Return me to her and she will release them."

Kosta shifted and lifted Ramsey up by his hair. He'd like

to slash the man's throat now that he knew where Heli was and how to get her back, but he'd already accepted Ramsey's surrender and would not abuse it.

"Call Taryn and–" Kosta didn't get to finish his sentence because a 1961 purple Dodge Power Wagon truck crashed through the front entry way of the old Bay hotel.

The truck bed was filled to the brim with the women who'd been captured by the Bay pack and they were armed to the teeth with all manner of weapons including some hot pink tasers. Selena Troika stuck her head up over the top of the cab and pointed at Ramsey with daggers in her eyes. Ramsey had better run. His mother with a vendetta was scary as shit. Mariya stuck her head out the passenger side and said, "I'm back, bitches."

Heli was in the driver's seat and looking so fierce it took Kosta's breath away. She spotted him and smiled so beautifully it lit up the dark night, or maybe it was simply the darkness in Kosta's own soul being driven away by the love in her eyes. She waved at him and blew him a kiss. "Hi honey, I'm home, and I brought friends for tea."

THE BUNNY AND THE WOLF

Heli was more nervous than the day she'd taken her final exams at culinary school. That had been the biggest and most important pivotal moment in her life up until now.

Tonight was infinitely more important. She and Kosta were going to be mated under the full moon in the wolves sacred ritual. Which involved outdoor sex and a whole lot of voyeurism. Heli could handle it because then the plans for a big ass wedding were going into full swing, which had Kosta quaking in his furry boots.

Selena had even booked the famous Willingham Weddings to do all the event planning, although Heli was still going to make the cake. She had so many plans and it was going to be a ton of fun. Now that Kosta was the alpha of the Bay and Fire Island packs, which Heli totally thought they should rename to something new and better, they were going to restore the old Bay hotel to its former glory.

The hotel would still be their pack house, but it would also be a place for packs to gather and have meetings to sort out their differences. Kosta wanted the war to end and he was working toward finding peace among the packs instead of them having to battle it out.

She was so proud of him and the work he was doing. He'd even invited the other packs he'd already made relationships with to come to the mating ceremony tonight in their shiny new sacred circle on the beach. It was a big move according to Selena. Packs usually kept their mating ceremonies to themselves, Tonight was kind of a big deal to all of wolfdom.

Thus, the nerves.

"*Ponchik,* you look a little pale. Doesn't she look pale, Selena?" Mariya had pulled all the women participating in the ritual tonight into her suite for a pre-ceremony drink. Thank goodness. Heli needed a stiff shot of anything alcoholic to help calm the storm of butterflies in her belly.

"Weren't we all on our mating nights?" Selena winked at Heli and lifted her flute of champagne to her. "You'll be fine."

She gulped the champagne down in two seconds flat. That helped her blurt out her biggest worry. "But everyone will be staring at us and my big bare ass that's going to be glowing as bright as the moon."

Gal grinned at her. "I promise, once you're in Kosta's

arms, you won't even notice anyone else is around. That's the magic of it all."

She understood that kind of magic. She felt it every time she was in Kosta's arms. Okay, fine, she could concede that part but there was one more thing bothering her. A lot. "I wish Zara was here."

Selena refilled Heli's glass and gave her a soft smile. "I know you do, but Doc says she'll be back up and around in no time. He's a good healer, she'll be fine."

Heli didn't know about that. She'd visited Zara every day in Doc's secret little hospital for shifters. Not once had her sister even said hello. Her eyes were blank and she remained completely silent all the time. That scared Heli more than any wolf war.

A timid knock sounded on the suite's door, and Violet stuck her head in. "Kosta said to tell you it's time."

Violet had become a different person after Decker's death. Her bravado had disappeared and a new quiet shy woman had emerged. As the pack's new matriarch, Heli was doing her best to help each of the women who'd decided to stay with the pack get the counseling and care they deserved. Many had been marked and developed abilities but had been hiding it all for fear of being used like Violet.

She waved the woman in. "Thanks, Vi. Do you want to come in and have a drink with us?"

"No, thank you. I'm going to... umm, I've got to... okay, bye." Violet shut the door gently and Heli heard her footsteps retreat all the way to the end of the hall where her room was. She spent most of her time there and Heli wouldn't force Violet to do anything she didn't want to, ever again.

Kosta had been right when he said her senses would become more acute. These days Heli could hear everything, smell things she'd never smelled before, and she'd developed a new taste for strawberries. Still no meat though. Gross.

Except for bacon. Who knew bacon went so well with everything in the whole wide world. She was totally making a maple bacon cake for their wedding.

Heli closed her eyes for a second to envision her cake and sparkles and rainbows went nuts behind her eyelids. Uh-oh. She was having another vision. Most of the time her visions were nothing special, like what she was going to make for dinner or who was coming to visit. She had seen one with Taryn Crescent standing at the top of a hill with a wolf's head in one hand. That one was weird.

The vision forming now wasn't like that.

She was running through the wooded area around the Bay and Kosta's big black wolf was at her side. Heli wasn't much of a runner, but this felt amazing. She looked down at her feet and almost tripped. They weren't feet. They were paws.

Holy cannolis filled with guacamole. She was a wolf.

"Heli? Earth to Heli, come in Heli." Selena's voice filtered into the vision and Heli opened her eyes.

"Whoa. That was awesome." She could hardly wait to tell Kosta and see when it was going to come true.

"What did you see?" Selena asked.

This one was for her and Kosta first. Selena and the others would find out about it later. "I'll tell you about it later. Let's get to the mating ceremony."

Mariya directed their little party through the woods to a secluded beach. The Bay's sacred circle had been over grown and it had taken them all a good week to uncover it. But now it was a beautiful area with trees on one side, the sea on the other, where the moon shone down on them and threw a million sparkles out over the water.

They passed dozens of men and women along the way and Heli greeted as many as she could. She wanted to do a good job being the new matriarch. As they approached the clearing, the people split and formed a path for her. Many whispered well wishes to her as she passed and it all felt so very special.

It was nothing compared to the moment she saw Kosta. He was standing at the center of the circle looking up at the moon in the sky, and he was glowing. Not just from happiness, like he was the moon and she was basking in the light reflected from him. Her chest constricted with how beautiful and proud he was like this.

Heli glanced around to see if anyone else noticed, but no one else seemed to. Selena did give her a sly smile though, then shooed her with her hands to go and enter the circle and be with her mate. Heli didn't need to be told twice.

She stepped into the moonlight and Kosta's eyes went immediately to her. They went wide, like he was seeing her for the first time ever, and then he smiled. He held out his hand to her and she hurried over to be with him.

'Hello, *zaika*." He swallowed hard and licked his lips like he wanted to eat her up. She hoped he did. "You glow so beautifully in the moonlight for me."

"I'm glowing? So are you." She put her hand on his cheek and saw the shimmer of her own skin when she touched him.

"My mother tells me only true mates can see each other's glow under the light of the full moon. I didn't believe her until now." Kosta bent and kissed her soft and sensually. "I'm so happy I was wrong."

"There's so much about being a shifter's mate I have to learn." She had to admit she was nervous about it, but with Kosta by her side, she was also excited.

"As I have a lot to learn about being an alpha." He took her hand from his face and kissed her fingers. "You're already an amazing mate and pack matriarch, love."

He was being so sweet. "You are adorable, but you know you don't have to be the alpha for me. I still like that naughty wolf I fell in love with who likes to fool around."

Kosta grinned and his eyes glowed a brilliant purple. Gone was the Troika blue. This new color emerged and spread to all the wolves he now ruled over. "For you, I will be both."

Heli hoped her eyes would be purple like that too when she became a wolf like him. She wouldn't know until that happened. "Good. I like both."

"Are you ready?" Kosta slid the collar of the silky white

robe she wore to the side and exposed the mark he'd given her. It too glowed in the moonlight, but not just white like the moon. It also had the soft purple sheen of his eyes.

"Make me yours again, Konstantin. Make me yours forever." Heli dropped the robe to the ground and pulled Kosta down for a kiss. She swept her tongue into his mouth to let him know he didn't have to hold back. She always wanted all of him.

With their kiss, howls sounded in the night air. Heli knew that was the signal to the rest of the wolves there that the ceremony had begun and they too could search for their mates in the sacred circle.

But Gal was right. She barely noticed.

Kosta laid her down on her robe to protect them both from the sand, and spread her legs wide with his. He reached between them and groaned when his fingers met her wet heat. She he was always ready for him, but these last weeks, she was aching and needy for his touch all the damn time. He kissed her, thrusting his tongue into her mouth and his cock into her pussy not making either of them wait to be joined.

Heli loved the way he filled her and it wasn't long before they were both breathing hard and close to coming. "Bite me, Kosta. Bite me, like when you marked me. I want to feel all of you again."

His wolf flashed through his eyes at her request and he buried his face in the crook of her shoulder. His hips pumped, he thrust into her so deep and bit her shoulder, sinking his fangs into her flesh. The pleasure of being taken by him so primally again skyrocketed her into an intense orgasm that dragged Kosta along for the ride.

He growled and spilled his seed into her. His cock grew thick and the knot locked their bodies together like it had since he'd marked her. "I love you Heli. Forever and always."

"Forever, Kosta. I'll love you forever too." Heli wrapped her arm around his shoulders and her legs around his waist, never wanting their bodies to part. She loved the way his wolf took over and he got all growly and possessive of her and her body when they were together like this. Every girl should get herself a wolf who could knot the hell out of her.

Kosta kissed his way along her neck, up her jaw, and then kissed her mouth for a very long time. When their bodies were replete and his wolf released the knot, satisfied she was claimed once again, he stared down into her eyes.

"Your eyes Heli. Your eyes are glowing purple." His voice was shocked, but pleased too.

Heli grinned up at him. "I think I have a surprise. Move over and watch this." She hoped she was right about this and didn't end up looking like a weirdo doing aftersex yoga.

She got onto her hands and knees and let a new warmth flow through her, the heat Kosta had given her from his heart and soul, poured through her. She howled up at the moon and for the first time felt her bones creak and crack, her skin split and her vision change.

Heli looked over at Kosta, who had also shifted and said, *Ouch. You didn't tell me it was gonna hurt like that.*

Sorry, zaika. *I would have warned you if I knew you were going to shift. I didn't think you would. No other humans have developed both a psychic ability and be able to shift. You are one special mate.* He gave her a sloppy lick across her muzzle.

Aww, babe. That's so sweet. Heli plopped down on her butt and swished her tail. *Now can you teach me how to move this weird body?*

Kosta pushed his head against her side and knocked her clean over. Instead of teaching her to run that night, they snuggled together under the stars and moon, as wolves, and as mates.

Fated mates, forever.

***

A TASTE OF KINKY WOLF

Cursed~

NIKO LAY sweaty and naked under the full moon. He stared up at the goddess who'd done this to him and cursed her name.

He'd chosen to sacrifice everything to her. Keeping her and all of wolfkind safe were worthy causes. He should have been rewarded with an afterlife of fluffy clouds and mountains of bacon. Instead he had a broken mind and his ability to shift into his wolf...gone.

What was he supposed to do now?

Stop fucking feeling sorry for himself, for a start. So, he wasn't a wolf shifter. He wasn't an Alpha anymore either and would never lead his own pack into the future. So what if he'd given up everything good in his life, including his true mate?

His brothers were safe, mated to their true mates, and each had their own packs now. The Volkovs weren't going to pull wolfkind back into the dark ages, and that should be enough.

He'd done more than his duty. Pride in that should sustain him for a thousand years.

Niko's heart beat hard against his chest and his vision tunneled. Doc had said if the darkness swirled, he could just say he would think about it tomorrow and then find something else to focus on. Like he was some kind of spoiled Southern belle.

Nothing could steal his mind away when the plague of despair infected him. Killing his best friend wasn't exactly the kind of trauma he'd simply get over. That night haunted him, hunted him, horrified him.

He wouldn't think about that now. He wouldn't think about the Volkovs, Russia, or the tragedy he'd caused right now. He'd think about that tomorrow.

Only one other memory he could call on pushed away the attack of anguish threatening to drown him. He'd retreated into the gentle caress of this oblivion too often, using the warmth he found there like a drug. She was his crutch, a way to numb everything else. He wasn't ready for rehab.

Niko closed his eyes on the night, ignoring the pull of the full moon, for the brilliant beautiful glow of Zara. He let the bright light of the memory take over his mind. The tension in his muscles melted away, the specters of self-hatred receded, all replaced by her.

If only they were both still teenagers. If only he hadn't broken up with her when he left for Russia. He wouldn't think about that now.

His vision of her wasn't fuzzy or marred with age. She was as clear and crisp as 8K television just like she was every time he thought of her. She smiled at him, and he reached for her, needing so much to bask in her sweetness.

Only this time, her smile faltered, a flash of hurt and sorrow crossed her face, and tears flowed from her eyes. Niko reached to wipe them away. When he touched their wetness, his fingers were on his own face.

Zara wasn't the one crying. He was. Fuck. Not again.

Instead of reliving his favorite memory of their first night together so long ago, he was back at the battle for Kosta's pack. Back to lying on the ground, bleeding, waiting for Zara to recognize him. Seeing her held captive by that asshole, Ramsey Crescent, had nearly ripped his soul from his body. Especially knowing he couldn't do anything to help her.

He was helpless. So weak, so disconnected from everything he'd ever known... So alone.

Niko opened his eyes and filled his vision with the bright light of the moon. Even she had forsaken him. The pull of her magic, the urge to shift into his wolf, pulled on him from deep inside. When he sought out the beast within, it didn't answer.

Niko didn't deserve to have the wolf any longer. Not

since he'd abused his Alpha strength and power. Not since Russia. The depths of his misdeeds roiled in his chest and stomach, and he quickly rolled in the grass, hurling bile and acid into the leaves.

He stayed hunched over, dry heaving and gasping for air until, finally, the nausea subsided. It took a few more minutes for the ringing in his head and the cold sweat to recede. He deserved every second of his miserable existence, but he was damn tired of it.

Either he stopped wallowing in this stagnant and deadly misery, or he fucking did something about changing the destructive path he was on. Being the alpha of the Troikas was off the table. Without his wolf, pretty much anything he'd ever imagined for his own future was no longer an option.

Fine. But he wouldn't be a drain on his family. He could still be a productive member of the pack. His life would be that of a mere mortal now. Humans did lots of things wolves could do, too. Some of his best friends were humans.

Someone he loved was human.

Maybe, just maybe, if he could prove himself worthy, and make himself into a better man than he'd ever been a wolf, he could win her back.

That was probably too much to ask.

He would try anyway. He had to. At this point, it was either pull his head out of his ass, or wallow in the darkness surrounding him until he died. Real happiness may not be in the cards for him ever again, not with a vital part of himself missing, but winning Zara's heart back and seeing her happy might be as close as he could get.

A lump formed in his throat, and he had to swallow down the fear that he could pull the beautiful angel down into his own hell. He would have to guard her from his darkness, not let her see his true self cowering in the hidden places of his mind. Niko would protect her

If she would have him. That was no guarantee. It was a place to start, though.

In slow, measured movements, he got to his feet. One vertebra at a time, he stood up straight. The light of the moon was brighter now, neither clouds, nor Niko's own dark thoughts blocked the rays calling to his blood. He'd spent his last night as a wolf in her glow, so it was right that he took his final night before embracing a new human life to bask under her as well.

Tomorrow, in the sunshine, the full moon would be no more than it was to any other human. No, her light would now symbolize his rebirth as an ordinary, average Joe Schmoe. A Joe who had wrongs of the past to right.

Starting with the woman whose heart he broke.

If he had his wolf, he'd sneak over to the hospital where Zara healed from the wounds, both mental and physical, inflicted on her by those damn Bay Pack wolves. He would watch over her in her sleep and make sure no shifter ever bothered her again.

Think like a human, stupid. Humans didn't watch each other sleep unless they were creepy stalkers. That meant he would wait until a reasonable hour in the morning and go see her during normal hospital visiting hours.

He'd bring her flowers... ugh, bouquets were nothing more than dead plants. Fine then, a small flowering plant in a pot. His mother should know where he could get something like that in town. Niko had been in Russia for so long, he hardly knew his way around his own hometown anymore.

Sleepy Folk, the speakeasy bar his family owned, was still going strong, especially since Max had taken over the day-to-day operations. Maybe Niko could help out there. He was part owner. The bar was a safer choice than Kosta's club.

That place reminded him a little too much of the clubs he and Mik spent time in during the long, cold Russian winters. Although, The Naughty Wolf was a hell of a lot tamer than the BDSM clubs owned by the Volkovs.

Niko picked up his pace and jogged through the Reserve and back toward the pack house. No way he should be thinking about domination and submission and Zara in the same thought.

He broke into a run.

No way he should be thinking of Zara on her knees, wrapped in miles of red rope, her thighs spread, her pussy dripping wet for him.

Niko sprinted through the trees, letting the bushes scrape his legs and the branches slap his face, neck, and arms.

No way in hell should he even entertain the thought of

having her across his lap, her plump soft ass in the air, pink from his spankings, begging him to let her come.

The muscles in his body burned, his lungs matching the pain as Niko pushed himself to run beyond the bounds of his humanly form. Faster, harder, he had to push his body so he could stop thinking about hers and all the things he wanted to do to it. The forested area of the Reserve opened into his family's spacious backyard, and Niko gave one final burst of speed.

Wolves howled not far off, probably scenting his desperation. Max and Kosta patrolled their expanded territories along with their Enforcers. There wasn't much the patrols missed, and there was likely already rounds of gossip spreading through the ranks about him.

That was nothing new. Being the heir to one of the most powerful packs around had given Niko plenty of practice being in the spotlight of wolf culture. He'd been destined to be a star. How he had fallen.

All he wanted now was to fade into obscurity. Let everyone forget he'd been groomed to be the best of the best alphas. Because then maybe they also wouldn't remember he was the right-hand man of the Wolf Tzar, whose death had thrown their entire world into chaos.

Whose death was all his fault.

The one person who didn't give a shit was Zara. She hadn't even known about werewolves like him until recently. She'd probably be happy he wasn't a wolf anymore. One more reason he had to find a way to win her back.

Niko slammed into the wall of the pack house, using it to stop his momentum. He bent over, hands on his legs, panting from the effort and his frustration. His cock was just as hard as a few minutes ago and no amount of physical exertion was going to get rid of it.

Niko slipped quietly inside even though it was unlikely anyone was here this late. Another thing he'd have to adjust to if he was going to live his life as a human. Christ, he hadn't needed to keep daylight hours since graduating from high school. Even then he'd been a night owl and missed morning classes more often than not. Wolves were nocturnal, but he wasn't a wolf anymore, so he'd better get used to getting up at dawn and sleeping at night.

He headed for the shower already stroking his hard-on. He'd have to settle for living out his fantasies of dominating Zara, making her come and come and come, with his own hand around his cock. Getting those ideas out of his system before he went to see her at the hospital was imperative, and impossible.

The Zara he'd left eight years ago to do his duty to his family and all wolfkind, was a soft and naïve teenager who'd given him her virginity. Hell, he'd been just as young and inexperienced back then. A couple of years with the Volkovs had changed all that.

She would always be his shining angel of innocence. He could imagine the slap across the face she'd give him for even suggesting she let him tie her up, spank her curvy ass, pull her hair, all while making her pussy sing with want and need.

No. His Zara might get as dirty as allowing him to go down on her, but she was a missionary style partner. Thus, Niko would be, too. A vanilla human life was what would help him to start over.

He'd keep both of them safe and protected in the staid existence of non-supernatural everyday living. No more wolves for her, no more wolf for him.

That's what he wanted. It's what he needed.

Somehow, he'd convince himself of that because, as far as he could tell, being a boring, middle-class, average citizen was his only choice to stay sane and alive. Plus, Zara had been through more than enough excitement for most humans' entire lives. This would be what was best for her, too.

For her, he could do it. He could be ordinary.

ALSO BY AIDY AWARD

Alpha Wolves Want Curves

Dirty Wolf

Naughty Wolf

Kinky Wolf

Hungry Wolf

The Fate of the Wolf Guard

Unclaimed

Untamed

Undone

Undefeated

Dragons Love Curves

Chase Me

Tease Me

Unmask Me

Bite Me

Cage Me

Baby Me

Defy Me

Surprise Me

Dirty Dragon

Crave Me

Slay Me

The Black Dragon Brotherhood

Tamed

Tangled

Twisted

Fated For Curves

A Touch of Fate

A Tangled Fate

A Twist of Fate

The Curvy Love Series

Curvy Diversion

Curvy Temptation

Curvy Persuasion

The Curvy Seduction Saga

Rebound

Rebellion

Reignite

Rejoice

Revel

By Aidy Award and Piper Fox

Big Wolf on Campus

Cocky Jock Wolf

Bad Boy Wolf

Heart Throb Wolf

ABOUT THE AUTHOR

Aidy Award is a curvy girl who kind of has a thing for stormtroopers. She's also the author of the popular Curvy Love series and the hot new Dragons Love Curves series. She writes curvy girl erotic romance, about real love, and dirty fun, with happy ever afters because every woman deserves great sex and even better romance, no matter her size, shape, or what the scale says.

Read the delicious tales of hot heroes and curvy heroines come to life under the covers and between the pages of Aidy's books. Then let her know because she really does want to hear from her readers.

Connect with Aidy on her website. www.AidyAward.com get her Curvy Connection, and join her Facebook Group - Aidy's Amazeballs.

Printed in Great Britain
by Amazon

35858531R00108